THE INDETERMINATE RELATIONSHIP

CONSPIRACY OF COSMOS

BHUVI
DESTINY

Made with ♥ on the Notion Press Platform
www.notionpress.com

To the ever-evolving essence of human connections,

This novel is dedicated to the indefinable bonds that shape our lives, much like the title suggests—**"Indeterminate Relationship."** An indeterminate relationship exists beyond clear boundaries or simple definitions. It is fluid, dynamic, and ever-changing, much like the intricate dance of emotions and experiences we share with those around us. May this story remind us that some of the most meaningful relationships in life are those that resist labels, embracing the beauty and complexity of the unknown.

Indeterminate: The word "indeterminate" signifies something that is not precisely defined or established, characterized by ambiguity, unpredictability, and open possibilities. It reflects the essence of life's unpredictable nature, where outcomes are not always clear and paths are not always straight.

Relationship: A relationship encompasses the complex web of connections between individuals, marked by emotions, experiences, and mutual influence. It represents the bond that two people share, evolving through time, challenges, and shared moments, defining their unique journey together.

In "The Indeterminate Relationship," these two concepts intertwine to explore the unpredictable yet deeply meaningful connections that shape our lives. This book is dedicated to those who embrace the uncertainties of life, finding strength and beauty in the ever-changing tapestry

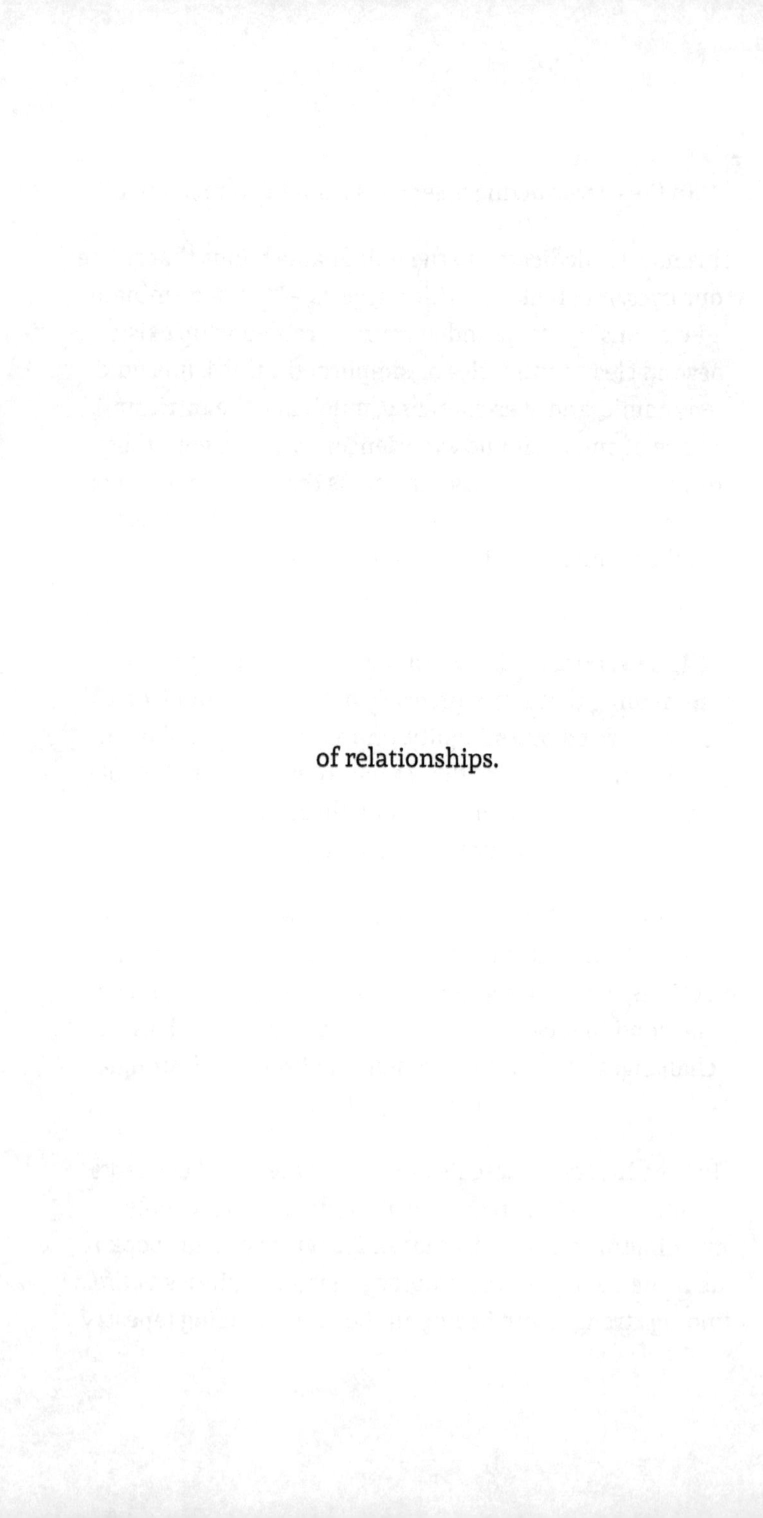

of relationships.

Contents

FOREWORD

The Indeterminate Relationship by Bhuvi is a profound exploration of the intricate and often unpredictable nature of human connections. In a world where relationships are expected to follow certain norms and trajectories, this novel dare to delve into the ambiguity and uncertainty that often characterize our most meaningful bonds. It is a captivating exploration of the nuanced and often unpredictable nature of human connections. As the title suggests, this novel delves into the complexities of relationships that defy simple categorization, reflecting the inherent uncertainty and depth that characterize our interactions with others.

"At its core, "The Indeterminate Relationship" challenges conventional notions of love, friendship, and loyalty. Bhuvi masterfully weaves a narrative that portrays the intricate dance of emotions, choices, and circumstances that define the bonds between individuals. Through richly developed characters and a compelling storyline, the novel invites readers to reflect on their own experiences and the multifaceted nature of their relationships. The term "indeterminate" implies a sense of ambiguity and open-endedness. In the context of relationships, it highlights the fluidity and evolving dynamics that often defy clear labels or definitions. Bhuvi's insightful storytelling captures this essence, presenting a world where the lines between different forms of connection are blurred, and the journey of understanding and acceptance becomes a central theme. These novel invites readers to embrace the unknown, to recognize that relationships, much like life itself, cannot always be neatly categorized or predicted. Instead, they are fluid, evolving with time, circumstances, and the choices we make—or don't make.

Bhuvi's narrative is a delicate balance of love, longing, and the complexities that arise when people connect on a level that transcends the ordinary. His writing is both poignant and thought-provoking, offering a fresh perspective on the timeless themes of love and connection. Whether you find yourself resonating with the characters' struggles or contemplating the broader philosophical questions raised by the narrative, these novel promises to leave a lasting impression. The characters in this story are not merely participants in a plot but are reflections of the very real and often messy emotions we all experience. Their journeys are a testament to the fact that relationships are as much about what is left unsaid as they are about what is spoken. In a world where relationships are often seen through the lens of rigid definitions, "The Indeterminate Relationship" reminds us of the beauty and complexity that arise when we embrace the uncertainties and embrace the journey itself.

This novel is not just a tale of love or connection; it is a meditation on the spaces in between—those moments of doubt, the pauses that carry weight, and the decisions that linger long after they are made. Through Bhuvi's eloquent prose and nuanced characterization, readers are invited to consider their own relationships, the indeterminate spaces within them, and the beauty that can be found in embracing life's uncertainties. As you turn the pages of *The Indeterminate Relationship, * you may find not only a compelling story but also a deeper understanding of the relationships that shape our existence. This novel is a tribute to the complex, unpredictable, and ultimately indeterminate nature of love and connection—a reminder that it is within the unknown that we often find the most profound truths. As you embark on this literary journey, be prepared to encounter a tapestry of emotions, dilemmas, and revelations. "The Indeterminate Relationship" is not just a story; it is an invitation to ponder the intricacies of the human heart and the profound impact of our interactions with one another. Bhuvi's work is a gift to readers who are willing to explore the intricacies of human relationships, with all their uncertainties and wonders. I hope you find this journey as enlightening and moving as I have.

With gratitude and admiration,

Preface

"The Indeterminate Relationship" is a story born from the depths of reflection on the complex nature of human connections. This novel is an exploration of the relationships that resist simple classification—those that exist in the grey areas, where emotions, intentions, and circumstances intertwine in unpredictable ways.

"The Indeterminate Relationship" is a story born out of a desire to explore the intricate and often unpredictable nature of human connections. As I penned this novel, I found myself delving into the depths of what it means to form, maintain, and sometimes lose relationships that do not fit neatly into predefined categories. I was driven by a desire to delve into the spaces between definitions, where relationships cannot be neatly labeled as just friendship, love, or something else.

Life often presents us with connections that challenge our understanding, leaving us to navigate through ambiguity and uncertainty. It is within these indeterminate spaces that the most profound experiences often occur. In writing "The Indeterminate Relationship," I aimed to create a narrative that resonates with readers on a personal level, inviting them to question, reflect, and perhaps see their own experiences mirrored in the lives of the characters. The story does not offer easy answers or neatly tied conclusions. Instead, it embraces the messiness of life and relationships, encouraging readers to find meaning in the uncertainty.

I sought to capture the essence of these ambiguous relationships. Through the lives of the characters, I aimed to portray the beauty and challenges inherent in connections that are not easily labeled. Their journeys reflect the reality that relationships can be multifaceted, evolving, and sometimes indeterminate.

"The Indeterminate Relationship" is a novel born from the intricacies and ambiguities that shape our most intimate connections. As I set out to write this story, I was drawn to the idea that not all relationships can be neatly categorized or understood through conventional labels. Life, after all, is filled with moments of uncertainty, where emotions and bonds defy clear definitions, leaving us to navigate the gray areas with a blend of hope, confusion, and courage. This novel is a journey into the unknown—a journey that many of us undertake in our own lives as we form and navigate relationships that defy expectations. It is a tribute to the courage it takes to embrace the indeterminate, to live in the questions, and to find beauty in the ambiguity

This novel explores the intersections of love, friendship, and loyalty, where the boundaries between them often blur, creating a tapestry of experiences that are both deeply personal and universally relatable. The characters in this story reflect the many facets of human relationships—complex, evolving, and sometimes indeterminate. They grapple with choices and circumstances that challenge their understanding of themselves and each other, revealing the unpredictable nature of human connection. This book is not just a story about love or friendship; it is a reflection on human experience. It is an exploration of the ties that bind us, the choices we make, and the impact of those choices on our lives and the lives of others. As you read, I hope you find yourself immersed in the characters' struggles, triumphs, and moments of introspection. As you read this novel, I, further, invite you to reflect on the relationships in your own life that may resist easy categorization. Perhaps you will recognize the moments of doubt, the unexpected twists, and the quiet revelations that shape your own connections with others. My hope is that this story resonates with you on a personal level, offering both insight and solace as you navigate the indeterminate paths of your own relationships. The story is not about finding definitive answers, but rather about embracing the journey of discovery, growth, and acceptance.

The characters in this story are a reflection of the many shades of human emotion and interaction. They face dilemmas that are both unique and universal, reminding us that the paths we take in our relationships are rarely straightforward. The novel seeks to capture the essence of those moments when clarity eludes us, and we are left to grapple with the complexities of our feelings and the choices they compel us to make. The concept of an indeterminate relationship speaks to the fluidity and complexity of our interactions. We live in a world where labels such as "friend," "lover," or "family" are often applied to define our bonds. However, life rarely adheres to these clear distinctions. Instead, we navigate a web of emotions, experiences, and connections that defy simple classification. In writing "The Indeterminate Relationship," I wanted to capture the essence of these uncertain spaces, where the true depth of a relationship is often revealed not through certainty, but through the very ambiguity that surrounds it.

I am grateful to everyone who has supported me throughout this creative process. To my family, especially Uma, your encouragement and patience have been my greatest sources of strength. To my readers, thank you for embarking on this journey with me. Your willingness to embrace the uncertainties of life and relationships is what makes this exploration worthwhile.

"The Indeterminate Relationship" is a labor of love, reflection, and discovery. It is my hope that it resonates with you, challenges your perceptions, and ultimately, enriches your understanding of the intricate web of connections that shape our lives. May "The Indeterminate Relationship" serve as a reminder that the most meaningful connections are often those that cannot be fully defined yet are deeply felt. Thank you for joining me on this journey.

Bhuvi

Acknowledgements

"The Indeterminate Relationship" is the result of a journey filled with support, inspiration, and encouragement from many incredible individuals. It is with deep gratitude that I acknowledge those who have contributed to the creation of this novel.

First and foremost, my heartfelt thanks to Uma, whose unwavering belief in me and this project has been a constant source of motivation. Your patience, love, and understanding have allowed me the space and time to bring this story to life. This novel is as much yours as it is mine.

To my children, your curiosity and boundless energy remind me daily of the wonder and complexity of human relationships. Thank you for being my inspiration and for filling my life with joy.

A special thanks to my parents-in-law for their invaluable support, taking care of our home and allowing me the freedom to focus on my writing. Your presence has been a blessing, and I am deeply grateful.

To my readers, your encouragement and feedback have been instrumental in shaping this story. Your engagement with my work fuels my passion for writing, and I am thankful for the community we have built together.

Lastly, to every person who has ever touched my life and influenced my understanding of relationships—whether through friendship, love, or shared experiences—this novel is a reflection of the lessons learned from each of you. Your stories, in some way, live within these pages.

Thank you all for being a part of this journey. "The Indeterminate Relationship" would not have been possible

without your support.

Bhuvi

Prologue

In the quiet moments between dusk and dawn, when the world is wrapped in the soft embrace of uncertainty, the true nature of relationships often reveals itself. It is in these indeterminate spaces, where love, friendship, and loyalty intertwine, that the heart's most profound questions arise. In the intricate dance of human relationships, the boundaries between love, friendship, and loyalty are often more fluid than we care to admit. These connections, so vital to our sense of self and belonging, rarely fit neatly into predefined categories. Instead, they weave a complex tapestry of emotions and experiences, each thread interlacing with the others to form a portrait of our shared humanity. Also, in the quiet corners of our lives, where the heart's whispers often go unheard, we encounter the delicate dance of human connection. It is here, amidst the subtle interplay of emotions and the intricate weave of experiences, that the true essence of relationships unfolds. "The Indeterminate Relationship" is a journey into these very spaces where love, friendship, and loyalty intersect, often blurring the lines between them and creating a rich, textured tapestry that both entangles and enriches us.

This novel begins in such a moment, where the boundaries between emotions blur, creating a complex tapestry of experiences that reflect the intricate dance of human connection. Here, relationships are not defined by clear lines or easy labels but are instead shaped by the choices we make and the circumstances that challenge our understanding of ourselves and each other. In this novel, you will meet characters who navigate the labyrinth of their own hearts and minds, each struggling to define their connections amidst a backdrop of uncertainty and evolving dynamics. These individuals are, although bounded by the rigid definitions that society often imposes but are instead getting shaped by the fluidity of their interactions and the complex emotions that come with them. In the intricate dance of human relationships, the boundaries between love, friendship, and loyalty are often more fluid than we care to admit. These connections, so vital to our sense of self and belonging, rarely fit neatly into predefined categories. Instead, they weave a complex tapestry of emotions and experiences, each thread interlacing with the others to form a portrait of our shared humanity.

"The Indeterminate Relationship" delves into this very fabric of human connection, exploring the intersections where love and friendship blur, where loyalty is tested, and where the lines between them become indistinguishable. This novel invites you to witness the myriad ways in which relationships evolve and shift, revealing their depth and complexity in unexpected ways. Love, friendship, and loyalty are not presented here as distinct and separate entities but as interconnected threads that weave together to form the fabric of our lives. As you turn these pages, you will witness how the boundaries between these facets of relationship can blur and shift, revealing the unpredictable nature of human connection. Choices made in moments of vulnerability, conflicts arising from unmet expectations, and the quiet epiphanies that alter perceptions—these are the elements that will shape the narrative and illuminate the indeterminate spaces we all navigate. It further invites you to step into this world, where the lines between love, friendship, and loyalty are fluid, and where every choice holds the potential to alter the course of a relationship. It is a story that speaks to the heart, reminding us that the most significant connections are often those that cannot be easily understood or defined, yet they are the ones that shape who we are.

Through the lens of these characters, "The Indeterminate Relationship" invites you to reflect on your own experiences. It challenges you to embrace the ambiguity that often accompanies our interactions and to find meaning in the evolving and sometimes contradictory nature of our bonds with others. As you turn these pages, you will meet characters who navigate this delicate terrain, grappling with the unpredictable nature of their bonds. They will face dilemmas that force them to confront their deepest fears and desires, revealing the true complexity of their connections. These characters are not merely figments of imagination; they are reflections of the universal struggle to find meaning and clarity in the relationships that define our lives. As you turn these pages, you will encounter characters who reflect the diverse facets of our own lives—the friends who become more like family, the loves that defy easy definitions, and the loyalties that challenge our deepest convictions. Their journeys are not straightforward; they are marked by uncertainty and transformation, as they grapple with choices and circumstances that question their understanding of themselves and each other.

In this world, relationships are not static or easily categorized. They are dynamic and often indeterminate, shaped by the unpredictable nature of human connection. As these characters navigate their intertwined lives, they confront the delicate balance between certainty and ambiguity, discovering that the most profound connections are often those that resist simple explanations. "The Indeterminate Relationship" is a reflection on the beauty and complexity inherent in our most cherished bonds. It is a reminder that while we may strive for clarity and definition, it is in the embrace of uncertainty that we often find the truest depth of our relationships. So, as you embark on this journey through the lives of these characters, may you find resonance in their struggles, revelations, and moments of profound connection; may you find echoes of your own relationships within these pages, and may the story resonate with the complexities and beauty of the connections that define us.

Welcome to a journey where the familiar becomes unfamiliar, where certainty gives way to ambiguity, and where the true nature of relationships is explored in all its beautiful complexity. This is a story of love, of friendship, of loyalty—but most of all, it is a story of the indeterminate, where anything is possible, and everything is intertwined. Welcome to a story where love, friendship, and loyalty intermingle in ways that challenge and inspire, offering a mirror to our own experiences and a celebration of the indeterminate nature of our most cherished relationships. Welcome to a world where the boundaries of love, friendship, and loyalty blur, creating a mosaic of experiences that are as personal as they are universal.

Bhuvi

I

Conspiracy of Cosmos

The universe has its way of weaving connections, often in the most unexpected places and moments.

For Raina, it was the Seminar Hall at IIT Chennai, a place she had entered with a singular focus: to present her groundbreaking paper, "Mathematical Modelling of Photonic Mass." Raina had always believed in the subtle power of the universe, the unseen threads that weave together the fabric of our lives. On a warm summer morning, as she stepped onto the sprawling campus of IIT Chennai, she couldn't help and not even felt that the cosmos had conspired to bring her here. The rustling leaves, the distant hum of academic fervor, and the palpable energy of the place seemed to welcome her.

She clutched her presentation materials tightly, her heart a mixture of excitement and nerves. Her paper, "Mathematical Modelling of Photonic Mass," was the culmination of years of research and sleepless nights. It was her passion, her contribution to the world of theoretical physics, and today, she would present it to some of the brightest minds in the field.

Raina is a brilliant and driven post-doctoral researcher in Mathematics, with a PhD in Photonics. Her academic journey has been marked by a relentless pursuit of knowledge and an innate curiosity about the world around her. Growing up, Raina always found herself drawn to the abstract beauty of mathematics, seeing it as the language of the universe. This passion eventually led her to the field of photonics, where she discovered the fascinating interplay between light and matter.

Raina is known for her sharp intellect and meticulous attention to detail, qualities that have earned her respect in the academic community. Her research, particularly in the area of Mathematical Modelling of Photonic Mass, has garnered significant attention for its innovative approach and potential implications in theoretical physics. Despite her achievements, Raina remains humble and deeply committed to her work, always striving to push the boundaries of what is known.

Beyond her academic pursuits, Raina is introspective and contemplative, often pondering the deeper questions of life. She believes in the interconnectedness of all things and sees the universe as a vast, intricate web where every action and decision have a ripple effect. This worldview shapes not only her research but also her approach to relationships and personal connections. Though dedicated to her work, Raina carries a quiet longing for something more—an undefined yearning for connection, perhaps, or a deeper understanding of her place in the cosmos. This makes her open to the unexpected, willing to embrace the unknown, and ready to explore the indeterminate paths that life presents.

Little did she know that this hall, filled with the quiet hum of academic minds and the sterile scent of polished wood, would be the stage for a meeting that would forever alter the course of her life. As she entered the hall, she was struck by the quiet buzz of anticipation that filled the room. Attendees were settling into their seats, flipping through programs, and exchanging polite nods with colleagues. The room was large, yet intimate in its design, with rows of seats descending towards a central stage where the podium stood, ready for the next speaker.

The seminar was a prestigious one, attracting scholars and researchers from across the country, all eager to share and absorb the latest advancements in their fields. For Raina, a young physicist with a sharp mind and a relentless drive, this was an opportunity to showcase years of dedication and countless hours spent refining her theories. The concept of photonic mass—a seemingly paradoxical idea that light, though massless in its traditional understanding, could exhibit mass under certain conditions—was a topic that had captivated her for years. Today, she was here to present her findings to an audience of peers and experts. The seminar hall was abuzz with activity. Academics and students mingled, exchanging ideas and pleasantries. As Raina entered, she scanned the room for a familiar face but found none. It was then that she noticed him—Raj—standing at the front, speaking with another committee member. His demeanor was calm and composed, a sharp contrast to her inner whirlwind.

Among the sea of faces, one caught her attention—a middle aged man with an air of calm confidence, moving through the crowd with a quiet authority. He was dressed in a simple yet elegant manner, a contrast to the more formal attire of many attendees. His name tag read "Raj," and it indicated his role as a member of the organizing committee. Raina noticed how he seemed to be everywhere at once, ensuring that everything was running smoothly, from the technical equipment to the seating arrangements. Raj was a member of the organizing committee, responsible for ensuring everything ran smoothly. His eyes caught Raina's as she walked in, and for a brief moment, he felt like she needed some help and at the same time a strange sense of recognition, as if he had known her from somewhere, perhaps in another lifetime. He watched as she settled into a seat near the front, her presence both commanding and serene. As the seminar commenced, Raj's responsibilities kept him occupied, but his thoughts occasionally drifted back to Raina. There was something about her that intrigued him, something that seemed to resonate with his own beliefs about the universe's hidden designs. As fate would have it, their paths crossed just as Raina was about to take her place in the front row. Raj, with his warm smile and easy demeanor, offered her a few words of encouragement, his tone professional yet genuinely interested. "Excited for your presentation?" he asked, his voice calm but with an underlying spark of curiosity.

Raina nodded, feeling a mix of nerves and anticipation. "Yes, it's a big moment for me." Raj's eyes lit up with understanding. "I can imagine. I've heard a lot of buzz about your paper. Photonic mass, right? It sounds fascinating."

She was surprised by his familiarity with her work but quickly realized that as a member of the organizing committee, he would have reviewed the abstracts. "Yes, it's been a challenging but rewarding journey."

Raj smiled again, this time with a touch of admiration. "I'm looking forward to hearing it. Best of luck."

With that, he moved on, attending to his duties, while Raina took her seat, her mind momentarily distracted by their brief encounter. There was something about Raj—his calm confidence, his genuine interest—that left an impression on her. But there was little time to dwell on it as the seminar began, and soon it would be her turn to step up to the podium.

As the event progressed, Raina found herself replaying their conversation in her mind, wondering why such a simple exchange had lingered with her. Was it merely the nerves of the day, or was there something more—a subtle hint from the cosmos that their meeting was not just a coincidence? When her name was finally called, she walked to the podium with steady resolve, her mind focused on the task at hand. Yet, in the back of her mind, Raj's words of encouragement echoed, giving her an unexpected boost of confidence. She took a deep breath and approached the podium. The room fell silent, all eyes on her. She began to speak, her voice steady and confident, unraveling the complexities of her research with clarity and passion. Raj listened intently, captivated by her intellect and the elegance with which she presented her ideas. As Raina spoke about the mathematical underpinnings of photonic mass and its potential implications, she noticed Raj in the audience, his gaze unwavering. It gave her an inexplicable sense of reassurance, as if the cosmos itself was lending her strength through him.

The presentation concluded to enthusiastic applause. Raina felt a wave of relief and accomplishment wash over her. As she stepped down from the podium, Raj approached her, his expression warm and inviting.

"That was an impressive presentation," he said, extending his hand.

"Thank you," Raina replied, shaking his hand. Their conversation flowed effortlessly, touching on their shared passion for physics and the serendipity of their meeting. There was an undeniable connection, a sense that their paths had crossed for a reason beyond the seminar.

Raj is an accomplished Associate Professor in Photonics, recognized for his profound understanding of light-matter interactions and his innovative contributions to the field. From a young age, Raj was captivated by the mysteries of light, seeing it not just as a physical phenomenon but as a symbol of knowledge and discovery. This fascination drove him to pursue a career in photonics, where he quickly established himself as a thought leader and a mentor to many. Raj's academic career has been marked by a series of successes, from groundbreaking research to prestigious teaching awards. He has a natural ability to simplify complex concepts, making him a beloved figure among his students and colleagues. Raj is passionate about fostering the next generation of scientists, and he takes great pride in guiding his students through the challenges of academia.

Despite his professional achievements, Raj is not defined solely by his work. He possesses a deep appreciation for the subtleties of life, often reflecting on the philosophical aspects of existence. Raj believes that science and life are intertwined, with each discovery in the lab holding the potential to reveal new insights into the human condition. Raj is thoughtful, empathetic, and introspective, qualities that make him an excellent listener and a trusted friend. However, beneath his composed exterior lies a restlessness—a desire to explore the unknown and challenge the boundaries of his understanding. This drive often leads him to question not only the physical world but also the relationships and connections he forms.

As an Associate Professor, Raj has navigated the complexities of academic life with grace, yet he remains open to possibilities that lie beyond the structured environment of the university.

But as the conspiracy of the cosmos would have it, this was only the beginning. The boundaries between their professional collaboration and personal connection would soon blur, leading them into the indeterminate spaces where love, friendship, and loyalty intertwine, setting the stage for a journey that neither of them could predict. Little did she know, the connection forged in that seminar hall would soon grow, intertwining their lives in ways neither of them could have predicted. The journey ahead would challenge their understanding of themselves and each other, revealing the indeterminate nature of the relationship that was just beginning to unfold.

After the formal meeting in the seminar hall, where their paths first crossed, Raina and Raj exchanged a few more words before the seminar resumed. The conversation was brief yet meaningful, marked by a shared respect for each other's work. Raj, intrigued by Raina's insights on photonic mass, found himself wanting to continue the discussion. However, the demands of the seminar and their respective responsibilities kept them from delving deeper into conversation at that moment.

Raina, for her part, felt a subtle connection with Raj—a kindred spirit in the world of photonics. But as much as she was drawn to the prospect of further discussion, her schedule was tightly packed. She had to catch a flight later that day to return to IIT Kharagpur, where she was currently a post-doctoral researcher. As the seminar concluded, Raina gathered her materials and prepared to leave. Raj approached her one last time, offering a sincere compliment on her presentation and wishing her well in her future endeavors. Raina thanked him, appreciating his professionalism and warmth.

With that, Raina left the seminar hall, making her way to the airport. As she traveled back to IIT Kharagpur, her thoughts occasionally drifted back to the seminar and her brief interaction with Raj. Though their meeting had been formal and brief, it left an impression on both of them—a seed planted by the cosmos, awaiting the right moment to grow. Back at IIT Kharagpur, Raina returned to the familiar rhythm of her post-doctoral research, but she couldn't entirely shake the feeling that something significant had begun in that seminar hall in Chennai. Little did she know, this was only the beginning of a journey that would challenge her understanding of both her work and her heart.

II

Beautiful Chennai

The sun had just begun its ascent over the Bay of Bengal, casting a golden hue across the city of Chennai. The early morning light danced on the waters, reflecting the vibrancy and life that characterized this coastal metropolis. Chennai, with its rich history and modern charm, was a city where tradition and progress coexisted harmoniously, and for Raina, it held a special allure. Chennai greeted Raina with its familiar embrace as her flight touched down. The city's vibrant pulse was a stark contrast to the serene, scholarly environment of IIT Kharagpur. It was a place where the relentless energy of the streets met the calm of the sea, creating a unique blend of chaos and tranquility.

As Raina made her way from the airport, she marveled at the city's distinctive charm. The warm, humid air carried a medley of scents—spices from roadside eateries, the tang of salt from the nearby coast, and the occasional whiff of jasmine from a street vendor's stall. The streets were alive with the hustle and bustle of daily life, a dynamic backdrop to her contemplative thoughts.

As her taxi wove through the bustling streets, Raina looked out at the city she had come to admire. This wasn't her first visit to Chennai, but every time she returned, she found herself captivated by its unique blend of culture, heritage, and innovation. The city's rhythm, a mixture of honking vehicles, bustling markets, and the occasional temple bells, was a melody she had grown fond of.

The iconic Marina Beach stretched along the coast, its wide expanse of golden sand inviting early risers for a walk or a moment of solitude. Raina often wished she had more time to explore the city, to walk along the beach at dawn, or visit the ancient temples that stood as silent witnesses to centuries of history. But her work always demanded her attention, pulling her into the depths of research and academia.

The architecture of Chennai was a testament to its diverse history. Colonial buildings stood proudly alongside modern skyscrapers, while the narrow lanes of Mylapore offered a glimpse into the city's soul with their vibrant street markets and centuries-old temples. The scent of jasmine and freshly brewed filter coffee filled the air, mingling with the salty breeze from the sea.

The opportunity to present her work on "Mathematical Modelling of Photonic Mass" had been a significant one, and the experience had been both exhilarating and nerve-wracking. But now, as she prepared to leave the city once more, her thoughts kept returning to the brief yet impactful meeting with Raj.

Raina had always appreciated Chennai's intellectual vibrancy. The city was home to some of the brightest minds in the country, and IIT Chennai was at the heart of this academic pulse. It was a place where ideas were born and nurtured, where collaboration and innovation thrived. And in this vibrant academic environment, she had crossed paths with Raj—a meeting that, despite its formality, felt like the beginning of something significant.

With her flight back to IIT Kharagpur looming, Raina made her way to the airport, the images of Chennai's beauty lingering in her mind. Raina decided to take a detour before heading back to the airport as she received a message of delay of her flight.

She had always found solace in Chennai's coastal beauty, and today, she sought a moment of reflection by the sea. She drove to Marina Beach, a stretch of golden sand that stretched languidly along the Bay of Bengal. As she walked along the shoreline, the rhythmic sound of waves crashing against the shore was a soothing counterpoint to the whirlwind of her thoughts. The vast expanse of the ocean seemed to echo the limitless possibilities and uncertainties that lay ahead. Raina felt a sense of calm wash over her as she watched the sun dip below the horizon, casting a warm, golden glow across the water.

Seated on a bench, Raina allowed herself to relax, her mind drifting back to the seminar in Chennai. The brief but impactful encounter with Raj lingered in her thoughts. There was something about their conversation, the ease with which they discussed complex ideas, that had left a lasting impression. She wondered about the potential for future interactions, pondering the paths that might intersect once more.

The golden sands, the historic temples, the lively streets, and the serene beaches all blended together, creating a mosaic of memories that she would carry with her. And as the plane took off, Raina looked out at the city one last time, feeling a quiet anticipation for what the future might hold.

The following morning, as Raina prepared to return to her research at IIT Kharagpur, she felt a renewed sense of purpose. Her brief encounter with Raj had sparked a curiosity that she carried with her, a reminder that the world was full of unexpected intersections and possibilities.

As she boarded her flight back, Raina looked out at the sprawling cityscape of Chennai, knowing that her journey was far from over. The city had offered her more than just a brief respite; it had rekindled her sense of wonder and anticipation for the paths that awaited her.

III

Life Returns to Normal for Raj

Back in Chennai, after the seminar concluded and the brief but intriguing encounter with Raina became a memory, Raj returned to the rhythm of his everyday life. The seminar had been just another professional obligation, one of many that filled his calendar as an Associate Professor in Photonics at IIT Chennai. For Raj, life in Chennai was a delicate balance between his professional responsibilities and the quiet joys of family life. After the intensity of the seminar and his brief but memorable encounter with Raina, he returned home to the familiar rhythms of his everyday existence—a life that, despite its routine, brought him a deep sense of fulfillment. For Raj, life in Chennai was a carefully balanced routine, a tapestry woven from the threads of professional dedication and familial warmth. He returned to the familiarity of his daily life, where the vibrant hum of the city blended seamlessly with the comforting rhythms of home. Raj lived in a charming suburban neighborhood with his wife, Ananya, and their two children, Anya and Aarav. Their home, nestled amidst a cluster of flowering trees, was a sanctuary from the bustling energy of the city. Every morning, Raj would wake to the sound of birds chirping outside his window, a gentle reminder of the simple joys that life offered.

The warm, familiar scent of home-cooked food greeted him as he entered. His wife, Ananya, was in the kitchen, expertly juggling multiple pots and pans, her movements quick and efficient. Their two children, Aarav and Meera, were playing in the living room, their laughter filling the house with a comforting liveliness. Raj's life at home was a world away from the academic intensity of his work. His wife, Ananya, was the steady anchor in his life—a source of love, stability, and companionship. They had built a life together that was fulfilling in its simplicity. Ananya, an artist by profession, brought creativity and warmth into their home, contrasting Raj's analytical and methodical nature.

Yet, as he resumed his daily routine, the thoughts of Raina lingered in the back of his mind, a subtle undercurrent in the otherwise predictable flow of his life. Raj returned home after the seminar, leaving behind the vibrant discussions and intellectual exchanges of IIT Chennai. His thoughts, however, lingered on the brief but intriguing encounter with Raina. Despite the intense focus required for his academic responsibilities, he couldn't help but reflect on their conversation. Yet, as he walked through the door of his home, he was quickly reminded of the life that awaited him beyond the walls of academia.

Their mornings were a well-practiced routine. Raj would rise early, review his notes for the day, and prepare for his lectures, while Ananya tended to their two children, Aarav and Meera. The kids, full of energy and curiosity, brought joy and occasional chaos to their household. Aarav, the elder of the two, was already showing signs of inheriting his father's inquisitive nature, often peppering Raj with questions about science and the world around him. Meera, still young, was more inclined towards her mother's artistic sensibilities, spending hours drawing and painting with Meera.

After breakfast, Raj would head to the campus, leaving behind the domestic tranquility of his home for the intellectual rigor of the university. At IIT Chennai, he was a respected figure, known for his dedication to his students and his innovative research in photonics. His days were filled with lectures, meetings, and research, all of which he navigated with a calm efficiency. Despite the demands of his career, Raj always made time for his family. Evenings were reserved for unwinding at home—dinners with Ananya and the children, helping Aarav with his homework, and listening to Meera's imaginative stories. These moments were a cherished reprieve from the pressures of academia, grounding Raj in the simple joys of family life. Yet, amid this routine, Raj occasionally found his thoughts drifting back to the seminar and his brief interaction with Raina. There was something about the way she had presented her ideas, the passion in her voice, and the clarity of her thought that resonated with him. It was rare to meet someone who shared his level of enthusiasm for photonics, and even rarer to find that connection with someone outside his immediate circle. He wondered if their paths would cross again, perhaps in another seminar or collaborative project.

However, Raj was not one to dwell on possibilities that might never come to pass. He was a man grounded in the present, focused on his responsibilities to his family and his work. Life, as it was, was fulfilling, and he had little reason to question it. The encounter with Raina, though intriguing, was just a moment in time—one that would likely fade as new experiences took its place. As the weeks passed, life for Raj settled back into its familiar pattern. The hustle of lectures, the progress of his research, and the steady rhythm of family life filled his days. Yet, the memory of Raina and the seminar lingered, like a bookmark in a story that was not yet finished, waiting for the right moment to be revisited. For now, though, Raj remained content in his world, surrounded by the love of his family and the fulfillment of his work. The indeterminate possibilities of the future were far from his mind, as life in Chennai continued on, beautifully ordinary and quietly extraordinary in its own way.

Ananya days were filled with the laughter and curiosity of children, a reflection of her own nurturing spirit. Raj admired her dedication and the effortless way she balanced her career with their family life. Meera, their youngest, was a curious and imaginative ten-year-old. She had inherited her mother's love for learning and her father's inquisitive nature. Her room was a testament to her eclectic interests, filled with books, art supplies, and science kits. Aarav, the younger of the two, was a spirited seven-year-old with an endless supply of energy. He loved to tinker with gadgets, often shadowing Raj in the evenings, eager to understand the world through his father's eyes.

One particular evening, after a long day at IIT Chennai, Raj returned home to the familiar aroma of Ananya's cooking wafting through the air. The kitchen was a hive of activity, with Ananya at the stove and the children animatedly discussing their day at school.

"Welcome home, Raj," Ananya greeted him with a warm smile. "Dinner will be ready soon. How was the seminar?"

"It went well," Raj replied, his thoughts briefly drifting back to Raina's presentation. "We had some fascinating discussions. I met some interesting people."

Ananya nodded, her eyes twinkling with curiosity. "You always meet interesting people at these seminars."

As they sat down for dinner, the conversation flowed effortlessly. Anya excitedly shared her latest school project on solar energy, while Aarav enthusiastically recounted his adventures in the schoolyard. Raj listened attentively, his heart full of gratitude for these moments of togetherness.

After dinner, the family settled into their evening routine. Raj helped Aarav with his science homework, patiently explaining the principles of electricity, while Ananya and Meera worked on a craft project. The living room was filled with the soft hum of conversation and the occasional burst of laughter. Later, as the children prepared for bed, Raj and Ananya found a quiet moment on the balcony. The night air was cool, and the city lights twinkled in the distance.

"You seemed deep in thought during dinner," Ananya remarked, gently nudging him. "Anything on your mind?"

Raj smiled, appreciating her perceptiveness. "Just reflecting on the seminar. There was a paper presentation that really stood out to me—by a researcher named Raina. Her work on photonic mass was impressive."

Ananya looked at him thoughtfully. "It sounds like you found it inspiring."

"I did," Raj admitted. "It reminded me of why I love what I do. And it made me think about the future, about the potential for new collaborations and discoveries."

Ananya squeezed his hand. "I'm glad to hear that. It's important to stay inspired."

Raj crouched down to examine her artwork, his heart swelling with pride. "This is amazing, Meera. You're getting better every day."

They spent the next hour playing and laughing, the pressures of work melting away in the warmth of his family's presence. Raj cherished these moments, knowing how quickly time passed and how fleeting these years with young children could be.

As the evening wore on, Raj found himself slipping back into the rhythm of his daily life. After the children were tucked into bed, he and Ananya settled down in the living room, enjoying a quiet moment together.

"Anything interesting at the seminar?" Ananya asked, sensing that something was on his mind.

Raj hesitated for a moment before nodding. "There was one presentation that stood out. A researcher named Raina presented a paper on 'Mathematical Modelling of Photonic Mass.' Her work was impressive, and we had a brief conversation afterward. It's rare to meet someone who shares such a deep understanding of the subject."

Ananya listened thoughtfully, her expression supportive. "It sounds like you connected on an intellectual level. That's always refreshing."

"Yes," Raj agreed, though he couldn't fully articulate why the encounter with Raina had left such an impression on him. "It was just a brief interaction, but it made me think."

Ananya smiled, taking his hand. "You're always thinking, Raj. That's one of the things I love about you. But don't forget to take a break sometimes and enjoy the moment."

Raj squeezed her hand in return, grateful for her understanding. "You're right. I'm lucky to have you and the kids to keep me grounded."

As they stood there, side by side, Raj felt a deep sense of contentment. His life was a harmonious blend of professional fulfillment and personal happiness. The love and support of his family were the foundation upon which he built his career, and the moments of inspiration he found in his work only strengthened that bond.

IV

Back to Kharagpur, Something Amiss

Raina returned to the familiar corridors of IIT Kharagpur, feeling a strange mix of comfort and unease. The journey from Chennai had been uneventful. She had spent the flight organizing her thoughts, making notes on the next steps for her research on photonic mass, and reflecting on the seminar. She had even drafted an outline for a new paper that she was excited to start. Yet, as soon as she walked through the gates of IIT Kharagpur, a feeling of disquiet settled over her. Her apartment, a small but cozy space near the campus, usually welcomed her with a sense of peace. But that day, it felt strangely unfamiliar, as if something essential had shifted in her absence. She unpacked her suitcase mechanically, trying to shake off the feeling, but it lingered, like a shadow in the corners of her mind.

The next morning, Raina immersed herself in her work, hoping that the familiar rhythm of research would ground her. She reviewed her data, ran simulations, and prepared her notes for the upcoming week. But no matter how hard she tried to focus, she couldn't escape the nagging sense that something was out of place. It wasn't just a matter of distraction—Raina was used to balancing multiple thoughts and ideas at once. This was different. It was as though the very foundation of her work, her understanding of the world around her, had been subtly altered. She began to notice small things that seemed off: her experiments weren't yielding the expected results, her colleagues were distant, and even her usually reliable intuition felt unreliable.

The campus, with its sprawling greenery and intellectual buzz, had always been a place of solace for her. But as she resumed her daily routine, she couldn't shake off a lingering sense of something being amiss. Her research had always been her anchor, providing a sense of purpose and direction. Yet now, as she dove back into her work on photonic mass, she found it difficult to focus. The equations that once danced effortlessly in her mind now felt tangled and elusive. Even the laboratory, usually a sanctuary of precision and discovery, seemed to echo with a disquieting emptiness.

Raina returned to Kharagpur with a sense of anticipation, eager to dive back into her research after the stimulating seminar in Chennai. The sprawling campus of IIT Kharagpur, with its tranquil, tree-lined avenues and the quiet hum of scholarly activity, had always been her sanctuary. Here, she found the solitude and focus necessary to pursue her work—her passion, really—with the dedication it deserved. But as she settled back into her routine, something felt different. It wasn't immediately obvious; the change was subtle, like a quiet dissonance in an otherwise familiar melody. Her research continued, her days filled with equations, simulations, and late-night sessions in the lab. Yet, a lingering sense of unease began to shadow her work, a feeling that something important was missing, or perhaps out of place.

The first sign of this disquiet came in the form of a simple equation. One that Raina had solved countless times before, almost as second nature. But this time, as she worked through the problem, her mind wandered, losing its usual precision. She found herself staring at the numbers, the once clear logic behind them becoming hazy. Frustrated, she pushed her chair back and took a deep breath, trying to refocus. But it wasn't just the equations. In her interactions with colleagues and students, Raina noticed a subtle shift. Conversations that once flowed easily now felt stilted, as if a layer of detachment had settled over her. She caught herself more than once lost in thought, her mind drifting back to Chennai, to the seminar hall, to Raj.

Raina's colleagues noticed the change in her. Dr. Sharma, her mentor and a seasoned physicist, approached her one afternoon in the lab.

"Raina, is everything alright? You seem a bit distracted lately," he said, his voice tinged with concern.

Raina forced a smile. "I'm fine, Dr. Sharma. Just readjusting after the trip to Chennai, I guess." But it was more than just the readjustment. The seminar had sparked something within her—a sense of unfinished business, perhaps, or a subtle shift in her perspective. Her encounter with Raj, brief as it was, had left an imprint. She found herself replaying their conversation, analyzing his insights, and wondering about the possibilities their collaboration might have unlocked.

It surprised her how often she thought of him. Their encounter had been brief, formal, and yet it had left an impression that was difficult to shake. She found herself replaying their conversation, recalling the intensity in his eyes as they discussed her presentation, the way he seemed to understand her work on a level that few others did. It was as if the cosmos had conspired to place him in her path, and now, she couldn't help but wonder why.

One evening, as she sat in her small, cluttered office, the shadows growing long as the sun set, Raina decided to take a walk to clear her mind. The campus was quiet at this hour, with most students and faculty having retreated to their homes or hostels. She wandered along the familiar paths, her thoughts still preoccupied with the unsettling sense that something had shifted within her. The other evening, as she sat in her apartment, surrounded by stacks of research papers, Raina felt an overwhelming need for clarity. She decided to go for a walk, hoping that the fresh air would help clear her mind. The campus was quiet, the usual hustle of students replaced by the tranquil sounds of nature.

As she wandered through the familiar paths, her thoughts drifted back to her time in Chennai. The seminar, the vibrant energy of the city, and most of all, her interaction with Raj. There was something about their meeting that felt significant, as if the cosmos had indeed conspired to bring them together for a reason. As she walked, her mind kept returning to the equations that had troubled her earlier. She couldn't understand why she had struggled with them—they were foundational to her work, something she had mastered long ago. But perhaps that was the problem. Perhaps she had become too comfortable, too set in her ways, and this unsettling feeling was the universe's way of nudging her toward something new, something more.

Lost in thought, Raina found herself at the edge of the campus, where the buildings gave way to open fields. The night air was cool and crisp, the sky clear and dotted with stars. She looked up, seeking solace in the vastness above, but instead felt a pang of longing, a desire for something she couldn't quite name. Returning to her office, she tried to refocus on her work, but the feeling persisted. It was as though a door had been opened, and now she was aware of something beyond, something just out of reach. The thought of Raj lingered at the edge of her consciousness, a reminder that there was more to life than the equations and theories that had defined her world for so long.

Days passed, Raina knew she needed to find a way to reconcile these feelings, to make sense of the strange disquiet that had settled over her life. But for now, all she could do was continue with her work, hoping that the answers would reveal themselves in time. While walking to the office, lost in her thoughts, Raina almost didn't notice when she stumbled upon an old friend, Ananya, who was also a post-doc researcher in the mathematics department.

"Hey, Raina! Long time no see," Ananya greeted her with a warm smile.

"Ananya! It's good to see you," Raina replied, grateful for the familiar face.

They walked together, catching up on their research and life. Raina found herself opening up about her recent trip to Chennai and the sense of unease she had been feeling since her return.

"It sounds like you have a lot on your mind," Ananya said thoughtfully. "Maybe you need to give yourself some time to process everything. Sometimes, a change in scenery or a significant encounter can stir things up inside us."

Raina nodded, appreciating the wisdom in her friend's words. "You're right. I think I need to find a way to integrate these experiences rather than pushing them aside."

One evening, after another day of frustratingly inconclusive work, Raina decided to take a walk through the campus. The night was calm, the air cool and crisp. As she walked, she tried to clear her mind, hoping that the familiar paths would help her regain her sense of balance. But instead of comfort, the silence only deepened her sense of isolation. As she passed the campus library, she saw a light still on in one of the windows. It was unusual at this hour, and out of curiosity, Raina decided to take a closer look. Inside, she found an older professor she had met only a few times—a reclusive figure known for his unconventional theories and solitary nature. He was engrossed in a thick, dusty book, his brow furrowed in concentration.

Something compelled Raina to enter the library. The professor looked up as she approached, his expression unreadable. They exchanged polite greetings, and after a moment of hesitation, Raina found herself sharing her recent experiences—the inexplicable unease, the sense that something was amiss. To her surprise, the professor listened intently, nodding as if he understood. After a long pause, he spoke in a low, measured tone. "The mind is a complex landscape, Raina. Sometimes, it's not the world around us that changes, but our perception of it. When that happens, it can feel as though the very ground beneath our feet is shifting."

Raina considered his words. Was it possible that her own perception was causing this turmoil? The idea resonated with her, but it didn't bring the relief she hoped for. If the problem lay within her, then how could she find her way back to solid ground? As she left the library and walked back to her apartment, Raina felt no closer to an answer. The unease still clung to her, a persistent presence that refused to be ignored. Something was indeed amiss, and until she could identify what it was, Raina knew that her work, her peace of mind, and even her sense of self would remain unsettled.

As the days passed, Raina made a conscious effort to address the sense of disquiet. She revisited her notes from the seminar, reflecting on the discussions and insights she had gained. Gradually, the sense of unease began to dissipate. Raina found herself more focused and motivated, her research progressing with renewed vigor. She realized that the feeling of something being amiss was not a sign of failure but a call for growth and exploration. As she settled back into her routine at IIT Kharagpur, Raina felt a deeper connection to her work and a newfound openness to the possibilities that lay ahead. The cosmos, it seemed, had indeed conspired to guide her towards a path of greater understanding and discovery. And as she continued her journey, she felt ready to embrace whatever came next, confident in the knowledge that she was exactly where she needed to be.

The sense of something amiss grew stronger, tugging at the edges of her mind. Raina couldn't shake the feeling that her life was on the cusp of a change, one that she wasn't yet prepared for but could no longer ignore. The cosmos, it seemed, had more in store for her, and whether she was ready or not, the next chapter of her journey was about to begin. Raina's return to Kharagpur was supposed to be a smooth transition back into her routine, but from the moment she stepped onto the campus, something felt off. The familiar surroundings—the red-bricked buildings, the expansive lawns, the quiet hum of academic life—should have brought her comfort. Instead, they seemed to amplify a growing sense of unease that she couldn't quite pinpoint.

The unease grew as days passed. Raina found herself questioning things she had never questioned before—her research, her place in the academic world, and even the choices that had led her to this point. The confidence she had always taken for granted seemed to be eroding, replaced by a creeping doubt that she couldn't easily dismiss. Her colleagues noticed the change in her demeanor. Normally composed and focused, Raina now seemed preoccupied, her thoughts often drifting during conversations. Her closest friend and fellow researcher, Priya, asked if everything was alright, but Raina couldn't find the words to explain what she was feeling. How could she articulate a sense of unease that had no clear source?

The cosmos had conspired once again, but this time, it seemed to be working against her, pushing her into uncharted territory. As Raina wrestled with the ambiguity of her situation, she couldn't help but wonder if this was just the beginning of a larger, more profound shift—one that would challenge everything she thought she knew.

V

New Conspiracy - "Photonic Society of India" Conference

As Raina continued grappling with her sense of unease, an unexpected opportunity presented itself. An email arrived in her inbox, its subject line catching her attention: "Invitation to Speak at the Photonic Society of India Conference." The annual conference was a prestigious event, bringing together the brightest minds in photonics from across the country. Raina's initial reaction was one of excitement. Being invited to speak at such a significant conference was an honor and a testament to her work. Yet, as she read through the details, she couldn't shake the feeling that this invitation was more than just a professional milestone. It felt like another piece in the larger puzzle the cosmos seemed to be assembling around her.

The conference was to be held in Delhi, just a few weeks away. Her mind buzzed with possibilities—new connections, potential collaborations, and the chance to share her latest research on photonic mass. However, the lingering sense of disquiet made her wonder if there was another reason she was being drawn to this event.

Raina decided to dive into preparations, hoping that the focus required would help her regain her balance. She reviewed her notes, updated her presentation, and even conducted a few new experiments to strengthen her findings. The work was demanding but also provided a welcome distraction from her unsettled thoughts. As the day of the conference approached, Raina found herself both nervous and excited. She boarded the train to Delhi with a renewed sense of purpose, the familiar hum of the tracks beneath her a soothing constant. She spent the journey reviewing her presentation and trying to calm the flutter of anticipation in her stomach.

The Photonic Society of India Conference was held at a grand venue, its elegant halls buzzing with intellectual energy. Raina was greeted by familiar faces and introduced to new ones, each conversation a reminder of the vibrant community she was part of. The schedule was packed with sessions, workshops, and networking events, creating a dynamic atmosphere that both exhilarated and exhausted her. Raina's presentation was scheduled for the second day. Raina mingled with the attendees, engaging in discussions that ranged from technical specifics to broader philosophical implications of their work. It was during one of these conversations that she heard about a special session scheduled for the evening—a panel discussion on the future of photonics and its role in shaping technology and society.

Intrigued, Raina decided to attend. The panel featured some of the most respected figures in the field, including a few she had long admired. The discussion was lively and thought-provoking, touching on everything from theoretical advancements to practical applications. But what caught Raina's attention was a comment made by one of the panelists—a senior researcher who spoke about the need for a new approach to understanding light and its properties.

"The future of photonics lies not just in our current theories and models," he said, his voice resonating through the hall. "We must be willing to explore beyond the known, to question our assumptions and embrace the indeterminate nature of our universe." The words struck a chord with Raina, echoing her own recent struggles with uncertainty. As the session ended, she approached the panelist, eager to delve deeper into his ideas. Their conversation was intense and stimulating, each question leading to new insights. Raina felt a spark of recognition—this was the kind of intellectual challenge she had been yearning for.

Later that evening, as she walked back to her hotel, Raina reflected on the day's events. The conference had reignited her passion for her work and provided a new perspective on her recent unease. Perhaps the cosmos had indeed conspired to bring her here, not just to share her research, but to find the answers she had been searching for. As she prepared for bed, Raina's thoughts drifted back to Raj. She wondered if he had attended the conference and if their paths might cross again. The idea brought a small smile to her face. Regardless of what lay ahead, Raina felt a renewed sense of purpose and a readiness to embrace whatever the future held.

The second day of the Photonic Society of India Conference began like any other, with participants milling about, coffee in hand, exchanging ideas, and preparing for another day of intense academic discourse. Raina was still buzzing from the previous day's conversations and the stimulating interactions that had followed. She had her presentation today and a few more sessions lined up, and she was looking forward to a workshop on cutting-edge photonic technologies later in the day. The atmosphere in the conference hall was one of eager anticipation. Scholars and professionals gathered in clusters, discussing the latest developments and networking with peers. The buzz of excitement was palpable, everyone engrossed in the day's events.

However, the sense of normalcy was abruptly shattered just before the morning's keynote address. The overhead speakers crackled to life, and a voice, tense and official, echoed through the hall. "Attention, please. We have received information about a potential security threat. We request all attendees to calmly and immediately evacuate the building through the nearest exit. Please do not panic." A ripple of shock passed through the crowd. For a moment, there was silence—then the room erupted into murmurs of confusion and concern. People began moving towards the exits, some with hurried steps, others with more caution, as they tried to process what was happening. The calm, intellectual atmosphere had been replaced by a growing sense of unease.

Raina, who had been reviewing notes for her presentation, froze as the announcement registered. Her heart pounded in her chest as she quickly gathered her belongings and joined the stream of people heading towards the exits. The crowd was moving in an orderly fashion, but the tension in the air was palpable. As they exited the building, they were met by a swarm of security personnel and police officers, who were directing people to a safe distance from the venue. The conference center, once bustling with academic energy, now stood eerily empty, surrounded by flashing lights and barricades.

Outside, the attendees huddled in small groups, anxiously checking their phones for news and updates. Conversations shifted from technical discussions to worried speculations about the nature of the threat. The sense of intellectual camaraderie was replaced by a collective anxiety, everyone on edge as they waited for more information.

Raina stood apart from the crowd, trying to process the rapid shift from normalcy to chaos. She felt a mix of emotions—fear, confusion, and a lingering sense of disbelief. The idea that a conference, a place dedicated to the pursuit of knowledge and innovation, could be targeted in such a way was deeply unsettling. As she scanned the crowd, she noticed several familiar faces—colleagues, professors, and students—all sharing the same look of unease. Raina's mind raced, trying to make sense of the situation. Was this just a hoax, or was there something more sinister at play? The uncertainty gnawed at her.

Minutes felt like hours as they waited for updates. Then, the sound of sirens grew louder, and more police vehicles arrived. The area was quickly cordoned off, and bomb squad units moved into the building. The tension among the conference attendees was almost unbearable. Conversations had quieted, replaced by the low hum of worried whispers. Eventually, the loudspeakers crackled again, and the same authoritative voice announced, "We are currently investigating a bomb threat. Please remain calm and stay in the designated safe areas until further notice. Your cooperation is appreciated." The word "bomb" sent a fresh wave of fear through the crowd. Raina felt her stomach knot. She couldn't help but think of all the people inside the building just moments ago, how close they had been to potential danger. The thought was terrifying.

Hours passed as the authorities worked to secure the area. Finally, the announcement everyone had been waiting for came: "Attention, please. After a thorough search, we have determined that the threat was a hoax. The building is secure, and you may return to the conference center. We apologize for the inconvenience and thank you for your cooperation."Relief washed over the crowd, though it was tinged with lingering anxiety. People began making their way back inside, the earlier sense of excitement now replaced by cautious optimism. The conference would continue, but the experience had left a mark—a reminder of the unpredictable world they lived in.

As Raina re-entered the building, she couldn't shake the feeling that the day's events were part of a larger, more complex narrative. The cosmos seemed to be weaving yet another intricate pattern, one that blurred the lines between safety and danger, certainty and doubt. The rest of the day unfolded with a strange mixture of normalcy and heightened awareness. The sessions resumed, the discussions continued, but the shadow of the bomb hoax lingered in the background. Raina, like many others, found it difficult to fully concentrate, her mind replaying the events of the morning.

As the day wore on, the organizers made the difficult decision to postpone the remaining presentations. The unexpected bomb hoax and the subsequent evacuation had disrupted the carefully planned schedule, and it was clear that many attendees were still shaken by the morning's events. The conference's atmosphere, once filled with intellectual enthusiasm, now carried an undercurrent of unease that was hard to dispel. A formal announcement was made over the loudspeakers: "Due to today's unforeseen circumstances, the remaining presentations have been postponed. We understand the importance of these sessions and have decided to continue them at the upcoming Optics & Photonics Conference in Mumbai. We appreciate your understanding and cooperation."

There was a collective murmur of agreement among the attendees. While some were disappointed by the delay, most understood the necessity of the decision. The focus had shifted from academic pursuits to ensuring the safety and well-being of everyone involved.

Raina, like many others, felt a mixture of relief and frustration. The day's events had been a stark reminder of how quickly life could take unexpected turns, disrupting even the best-laid plans. Yet, she also felt a renewed determination to continue her work and share her findings when the time was right. As she packed her materials and prepared to leave, Raina found herself reflecting on the strange twists of fate that had brought her here. The cosmos, it seemed, had conspired once again—not just to bring her to this conference, but to remind her of the fragile balance between order and chaos, certainty and unpredictability. The postponement of the presentations felt like a pause in the narrative, a brief interlude before the story continued in Mumbai. The next conference, dedicated to Optics & Photonics, would now take on even greater significance, as it became the stage where the work interrupted in Delhi would finally be shared.

As Raina left the conference center and headed back to her hotel, she couldn't help but feel that the upcoming event in Mumbai would be more than just a continuation of what had been postponed—it would be an opportunity to reconnect, reflect, and perhaps uncover new truths in the ever-evolving field of photonics. The cosmos had set the stage once again, and Raina knew she had to be ready for whatever came next. On reaching her hotel that night, she couldn't help but feel that the cosmos was conspiring in ways she had yet to fully understand. The bomb hoax, though ultimately harmless, had shaken her, reminding her of the fragile nature of the world they lived in. It was another reminder that the boundaries between certainty and uncertainty, safety and danger, were often more indeterminate than they appeared.

In the quiet of her room, Raina reflected on the day's events. The conference had taken on a new significance—no longer just a professional gathering, but a place where the unpredictable nature of life had revealed itself. And as she drifted off to sleep, she couldn't help but wonder what new challenges and conspiracies the cosmos had in store for her.

Next morning, Raina knew it was time to return to her routine at IIT Kharagpur. The unexpected events of the day had left her feeling drained, both emotionally and mentally. She decided that the best course of action was to head back home, regroup, and prepare for the next phase of her work.

Without wasting time, Raina booked a flight to Kolkata, the nearest airport to Kharagpur. The process was quick and efficient, but the weight of the day's events lingered in her mind. As she packed her belongings and checked out of the hotel, she felt a mixture of relief and lingering unease. The promise of getting back to familiar surroundings was comforting, but the disruption had left a mark on her psyche. At the airport, the usual bustle of travelers offered a strange sense of normalcy. Raina moved through security, boarded her flight, and settled into her seat, hoping that the short journey would give her time to clear her mind. The plane took off smoothly, and as it climbed into the sky, Raina gazed out of the window, watching Delhi fade into the distance below.

The flight was uneventful, the hum of the engines and the occasional announcement from the captain providing a soothing backdrop. Raina's thoughts drifted to the postponed conference and the upcoming event in Mumbai. She wondered what new opportunities and challenges awaited her there, but for now, she was content to focus on the immediate future—returning to Kharagpur, reconnecting with her research, and finding a way to make sense of everything that had happened.

As the plane began its descent into Kolkata, Raina felt a sense of calm beginning to settle over her. The familiar landscape of West Bengal came into view, and she took comfort in the thought of returning to her work, her colleagues, and the routine that had always grounded her. After landing, Raina collected her luggage and made her way to the taxi stand. The drive to Kharagpur was familiar and uneventful, the passing scenery a comforting reminder of home. When she finally arrived at her apartment, she was greeted by the quiet stillness of the campus, a stark contrast to the chaos of the day.

As she stepped inside and closed the door behind her, Raina felt a wave of exhaustion wash over her. The events in Delhi had taken their toll, but now, in the safety and familiarity of her own space, she could finally begin to process everything. She unpacked her bags, set her work materials aside, and allowed herself a moment of rest. Raina knew that the challenges she faced were far from over, but for now, she was back where she belonged, ready to continue her journey—both in her research and in whatever else the cosmos had in store for her.

The Photonic Society of India Conference had been more than just a professional milestone—it was a turning point, a new conspiracy of the cosmos that promised to lead Raina to new discoveries, both in her work and within herself. The annual "Photonic Society of India" Conference was a prestigious event that gathered the brightest minds in the field of photonics from across the country. Held in various cities each year, it was a platform for researchers, academics, and industry experts to share their latest findings, discuss emerging trends, and forge new collaborations. This year, the conference was set to take place in Mumbai, and it promised to be one of the most significant gatherings in recent memory.

Life slowly returned to its familiar rhythm for Raina. Her days were filled with research, teaching, and the usual academic responsibilities. The campus, with its quiet, tree-lined paths and the steady hum of intellectual activity, provided a welcome contrast to the chaos she had experienced in Delhi.

Yet, despite the return to normalcy, Raina couldn't completely shake the thoughts of Raj. Their brief interaction at the Chennai Conference and a miss in Delhi conference, though formal and fleeting, had left an impression on her. She found herself thinking about him at odd moments—during quiet evenings in her office, while walking to the library, or even in the middle of her research. It wasn't just Raj as a person that occupied her thoughts, but the strange, almost fated way their paths had crossed in the seminar hall at IIT Chennai. These thoughts, however, remained just that—quiet musings that she didn't allow to interfere with her work. Raina was determined to focus on her research, to stay productive, and to prepare for whatever challenges lay ahead. But every now and then, a memory of Raj would surface, leaving her to wonder if their paths might cross again.

Days turned into weeks, and the Delhi conference began to feel like a distant memory. Raina buried herself in her projects, pushing forward with her work on photonic mass and contributing to various academic papers. Life moved on, but the cosmos had other plans. One day, as Raina was sorting through her emails, a subject line caught her attention: "Invitation to the Optics & Photonics Conference in Mumbai." Her heart skipped a beat as she opened the email. The message was from the organizing committee, officially inviting her to present her research at the conference that had been rescheduled following the disruptions in Delhi.

Raina felt a surge of excitement. The Mumbai conference was not only an opportunity to share her latest findings but also a chance to reconnect with the academic community. However, as she read through the details, another thought crossed her mind—Raj. Would he be there? The possibility brought a mix of anticipation and uncertainty. The invitation was clear: her presentation on "Mathematical Modelling of Photonic Mass" was to be a highlight of the event. The conference promised to be an even bigger affair than the one in Delhi, with more participants and a broader range of topics. It was an opportunity she couldn't pass up.

Raina accepted the invitation without hesitation, her thoughts a swirl of professional determination and personal curiosity. The cosmos had indeed conspired once again, drawing her back into the world of optics and photonics, and perhaps, into another encounter with Raj. As the days counted down to the Mumbai conference, Raina felt a renewed sense of purpose. She prepared her presentation with meticulous care, determined to make the most of this opportunity. But in the back of her mind, there lingered the question of what the cosmos had in store for her next. The stage was set for another chapter in her journey, one that promised not only professional advancement but also the possibility of unexpected connections and new conspiracies waiting to unfold in the vibrant city of Mumbai.

Raina received her invitation to present at the conference just a week after her unsettling return to Kharagpur. The news should have thrilled her—being asked to present her work on "Mathematical Modelling of Photonic Mass" at such a prestigious event was a testament to her standing in the field. Yet, the persistent sense of unease that had settled over her life since her return made it difficult for her to feel the excitement she knew she should. Despite her lingering doubts, Raina knew she couldn't pass up the opportunity. The conference would not only give her a chance to showcase her research but also offer a much-needed change of scenery. Perhaps the shift in environment and the intellectual stimulation of the conference would help her shake off the malaise that had been dogging her steps.

As the date of the conference approached, Raina threw herself into preparation. She refined her presentation, rehearsing her speech until it felt polished yet natural. She also reviewed the latest papers in her field, eager to engage with the cutting-edge ideas that would undoubtedly be discussed.

Meanwhile, in Chennai, Raj had also received an invitation to the conference. As a respected figure in the field, he was scheduled to chair one of the key sessions on the applications of photonics in next-generation technologies. He was looking forward to the event, not just for the academic discourse, but also because it offered a brief respite from the routines of his daily life. As the conference drew near, Raj found himself thinking about Raina again. Their brief meeting in Chennai had left a mark on him, and he was curious to see how her work had progressed. He wondered if she would be attending the conference, and if they might have a chance to continue the conversation that had been cut short at the seminar. The thought of seeing her again added a layer of anticipation to what was already an exciting event.

The day finally arrived. Raina boarded the flight to Mumbai with a mixture of nervous energy and cautious optimism. The city greeted her with its usual frenetic pace, a whirlwind of people and vehicles set against the backdrop of towering skyscrapers and the expansive Arabian Sea. The conference venue was a sleek, modern convention center located in the heart of the city, its glass façade reflecting the bustling energy of Mumbai.

The opening ceremony was grand, with speeches from luminaries in the field and a keynote address that set the tone for the days to come. As Raina mingled with other attendees during the breaks, she found herself gradually easing into the flow of the conference. The discussions were stimulating, the exchange of ideas invigorating, and for the first time in weeks, she felt a semblance of her old self returning.

Raj arrived at the conference with his usual calm demeanor, quickly finding himself surrounded by colleagues and students eager to catch up with him. He made his way through the crowded lobby, exchanging pleasantries and engaging in quick discussions about ongoing research projects. As he navigated the throng of people, his eyes scanned the room, searching for a familiar face. It was during the second day of the conference that their paths crossed again. Raina was heading to a session on theoretical advances in photonics when she saw Raj across the corridor. Their eyes met, and for a moment, the noise and activity of the conference seemed to fade into the background. They approached each other with smiles that held both recognition and a hint of surprise.

"Raina," Raj greeted her warmly, "I had a feeling I might see you here."

"Raj," she replied, her voice laced with a mixture of relief and curiosity, "It's good to see you again."

They fell into conversation easily, discussing the conference, their respective presentations, and the latest developments in their fields. As they talked, Raina couldn't help but notice how comfortable she felt around Raj. His presence had a grounding effect on her, a welcome contrast to the unsettling feelings that had plagued her in Kharagpur. Raj, for his part, was equally intrigued by Raina's insights. Her passion for her work was evident, and he found himself drawn to her intellectual rigor and the subtle intensity that underpinned her words. There was a connection between them that went beyond professional respect—a shared understanding of the challenges and triumphs that came with their chosen field.

As the conference progressed, Raina and Raj found themselves gravitating towards each other during sessions and breaks. They attended each other's presentations, offering feedback and discussing the implications of their work. The more they talked, the more they realized how much they had in common—not just in their professional lives, but in their broader perspectives on life, science, and the pursuit of knowledge. However, the undercurrent of something amiss in Raina's life was never far from her mind. Raina found herself lost in thought more often than usual. Her mind was occupied with something more intangible, something she couldn't quite name. She imagined how a conversation with Raj might unfold when she would tell him her feelings, sometimes picturing him listening with the same thoughtful expression he had worn during their brief meeting in Chennai. In her mind, she shared with him the strange unease that had settled in since she returned to Kharagpur. She explained how, despite her efforts to focus on work, she felt as though she was being subtly pushed toward something—an idea, a realization, or maybe even a decision she hadn't yet made. Raj, she imagined, would gently suggest that the intensity of her work might be the cause, creating an imbalance in her life. He would likely advise her to take a step back, to find a way to restore harmony between her professional and personal worlds. But deep down, Raina knew it wasn't just stress. There was something more, something she couldn't quite grasp but felt all around her. It was as if the cosmos was whispering to her, urging her to pay attention to something she had yet to see. The more she thought about it, the more these imagined conversations with Raj played out in her mind, the deeper she delved into her own thoughts. It was becoming harder to distinguish between what was real and what was merely the product of her introspection. Sometimes, in the midst of her musings, Raina would catch herself holding her breath, as if waiting for a revelation that was just out of reach. The sensation was unsettling—like breathing, but the breath wouldn't come. It was as though she was suspended between two realities, neither of which she fully understood. The feeling lingered, growing stronger with each passing day, pulling her further into herself, deeper into a space where logic and intuition intertwined. She couldn't help but wonder if the answers she sought would reveal themselves in Mumbai, or if this was just the beginning of a journey that would take her far beyond the boundaries of what she had ever known.

The conference came to a close with a grand dinner and awards ceremony, a celebration of the achievements and contributions of those in the field. As Raina and Raj sat together at one of the tables, surrounded by colleagues and the buzz of conversation, they both felt a sense of completion, as if something significant had been set in motion during the past few days. As the Mumbai conference drew to a close, Raina and Raj found themselves amidst a flurry of activity, colleagues, and acquaintances. The event had been a success, filled with insightful presentations and lively discussions. The two had managed to steal a few moments here and there to talk, sharing their thoughts on the latest research and their experiences since Delhi.

As the final day wound down, they knew it was time to return to their respective lives. Both felt a strong desire to stay in touch, to continue their conversations beyond the confines of the conference. They stood in the bustling lobby, surrounded by other attendees making their farewells, and promised to exchange contact information.

"I'll text you the details of my next paper," Raj said, reaching for his phone.

"And I'll send you some links to the latest studies I've been working on," Raina replied with a smile.

But in the chaos of the moment, as they juggled conversations and goodbyes with others, something inexplicable happened. They exchanged numbers with everyone else—colleagues, new acquaintances, even the hotel staff they had befriended—but somehow, not with each other. As Raina stood by the taxi stand, watching Raj disappear into the crowd, she felt a strange pang of regret. It was as if the cosmos had intervened once again, creating an odd barrier between them. She shook her head, trying to make sense of it, but the moment had passed.

Raj, too, felt a sense of incompletion as he boarded his flight back home. He replayed their conversations in his mind, wondering how they had missed such an important detail. There was an odd sense of inevitability about it, as though their connection was meant to remain just out of reach, at least for now. Both Raina and Raj carried on with their lives, diving back into their work, yet always with a lingering thought of the unfinished conversation. The cosmos, it seemed, had left a chapter unwritten, waiting for another moment in time to bring their paths together once more. There was an unspoken understanding between them that their connection had deepened over the course of the conference, and that this was just the beginning of something that neither of them could fully define. The conference, much like the seminar where they had first met, had been more than just an academic gathering. It had been another step in the intricate dance of fate, a new conspiracy of the cosmos that would continue to unfold in ways they couldn't yet foresee.

Raina returned to Kharagpur with a heavy heart. The sense of unease that had started to surface after the Delhi conference was now magnified. The missed opportunity to stay in touch with Raj gnawed at her, leaving her with an inexplicable sense of loss. It wasn't just about the missed contact; it was something deeper, something that had been growing within her since that first encounter in Chennai.

Life in Kharagpur resumed its usual pace, but for Raina, everything felt different. She threw herself into her research, trying to drown out the thoughts that kept creeping into her mind. But the more she tried to focus, the more distracted she became. Every little thing reminded her of Raj—their brief conversations, his thoughtful insights, the way he had looked at her as if he understood the turmoil she was going through. The pain she felt was subtle, almost elusive, but it was there, lurking beneath the surface. It was a pain born not just of regret but of something deeper—an unresolved connection, a conversation that had never reached its conclusion. She felt as though a part of her was missing, and no matter how hard she tried, she couldn't quite grasp what it was.

Raina's nights became restless. She would lie awake, her mind racing with thoughts and questions she couldn't answer. The strange feeling of being nudged towards something—a realization or a choice—had only intensified. It was as if the cosmos was pushing her toward an unknown destination, and she was powerless to resist. In the quiet of her apartment, Raina often found herself staring into the darkness, the silence pressing in on her. The pain wasn't sharp or overwhelming, but it was constant, a dull ache that refused to go away. She wondered if Raj felt the same, if he too was struggling with the same questions, the same sense of incompletion.

Days turned into weeks, and the pain remained, a constant companion in her life. Raina knew she had to move forward, to find a way to reconcile these feelings with the life she was living. But the path ahead seemed unclear, shrouded in uncertainty. The only thing she knew for sure was that something had changed within her, something that wouldn't be easily resolved. The cosmos, it seemed, had woven their fates together in a way that was both intricate and indeterminate. And as Raina continued to navigate this new reality, she couldn't shake the feeling that this was only the beginning of a journey that would take her to places she had never imagined, both within herself and beyond.

VI

The First Contact

Raj had been thinking about Raina more than he cared to admit. Their brief encounters at the conferences had left an impression on him, one that he found difficult to shake. The missed opportunity to exchange contact information with her weighed on his mind, especially as he continued to delve deeper into his research on photonic mass. He couldn't help but feel that their discussions could offer valuable insights, and perhaps even lead to a collaboration that would push the boundaries of their work.

The more Raj thought about it, the more he realized that he needed to get in touch with Raina. The topic of photonic mass was becoming increasingly important in his research, and her expertise in mathematical modeling was something he deeply respected. But beyond the professional reasons, there was a personal curiosity that nagged at him—a desire to understand the connection he felt during their conversations.

Determined to bridge the gap that had been left after the Mumbai conference, Raj decided to take action. He remembered that Mr. Swamy, one of his colleagues who had also attended the conference, had been quite impressed with Raina's work. Perhaps Swamy had her contact information.

Raj approached Swamy one afternoon in the faculty lounge. After some small talk, he casually brought up Raina's name.

"Swamy, do you happen to have Raina's number? We were supposed to exchange contacts in Mumbai, but somehow we missed it," Raj asked, trying to keep his tone light.

Swamy nodded, pulling out his phone. "Yes, I have it. She's brilliant, isn't she? Her work on photonic mass is really something. I'll send you her number."

Raj thanked him, feeling a sense of relief as Swamy forwarded the contact details. With Raina's number now in his possession, Raj took a moment to gather his thoughts. He wanted to approach the conversation professionally, focusing on the model reliability of photonic mass. Yet, a part of him was undeniably curious about how she had been since their last meeting.

Later that evening, Raj sat down in his study, phone in hand. He drafted a message, deciding it was better to reach out via text first.

"Hi Raina, this is Raj. I hope you've been well. I've been thinking about our discussions on photonic mass and would love to continue them. I've been working on the model reliability and thought your insights could be invaluable. Could we set up a time to chat?" He read the message over a few times, then hit send. As he waited for her reply, Raj couldn't help but wonder how the conversation would unfold, and whether it might lead to more than just a discussion about photonic mass.

The evening sun cast long shadows over IIT Kharagpur's campus as Raina sat in her office, the soft hum of her computer the only sound breaking the quiet. The day had been filled with routine tasks, but her mind kept drifting back to the conversation with Raj. The call had been both a welcome distraction and a source of new questions, and she found herself reflecting on it as she worked. Her phone buzzed on her desk, interrupting her thoughts. It was a message from Raj, confirming their earlier conversation and suggesting a time for a follow-up call to discuss the photonic mass model in more detail. Raina's heart skipped a beat. The prospect of continuing their dialogue brought a renewed sense of excitement, a feeling she hadn't had in a long time.

Later that evening, Raj was in his study, surrounded by papers and research materials. He had spent the day analyzing data and preparing for upcoming presentations, but his thoughts kept returning to his conversation with Raina. There was something compelling about their discussions, a sense of intellectual and personal connection that went beyond mere professional exchange.

As the appointed time for their follow-up call approached, Raj felt a mix of anticipation and nervousness. He hoped their conversation would provide the clarity they both sought, and perhaps shed light on the underlying currents that seemed to pull them together.

The phone rang, and Raj picked it up with a sense of eager expectation. "Hello, Raina."

"Hi, Raj. It's good to hear from you again," Raina replied, her voice warm and familiar.

They settled into their discussion with ease, their conversation flowing effortlessly from one topic to the next. Raj was impressed by Raina's depth of knowledge and her ability to articulate complex ideas with clarity. They explored various aspects of the photonic mass model, discussing potential improvements and addressing questions that had arisen since their last talk.

As the conversation progressed, Raj couldn't help but sense that there was more to their dialogue than just technical details. The way Raina spoke about her work, her struggles, and her reflections hinted at a deeper emotional layer. He decided to broach the subject gently.

"Raina, you mentioned before that you've been feeling uneasy since returning to Kharagpur. Have you had any breakthroughs or insights into what's been bothering you?"

Raina paused for a moment, considering her response. "I've been thinking a lot about that. The unease hasn't completely gone away, but talking with you has helped me feel less alone in it. I still feel like I'm being pushed toward something, but I'm not sure what."

Raj listened attentively. "Sometimes, it's not about finding immediate answers but about being open to the journey itself. Maybe this feeling is guiding you toward a new understanding or a significant change in your life."

Raina nodded, feeling a sense of validation in Raj's words. "I hope you're right. It's just that this feeling has been so persistent, and it's hard to ignore." Their conversation continued, shifting between professional topics and more personal reflections. As they spoke, Raina began to appreciate the way Raj's perspective offered a different lens through which to view her own experiences. It was as if their discussions were not only illuminating her current challenges but also paving the way for new insights.

By the time they ended the call, Raina felt a sense of clarity and connection that she hadn't experienced in a long time. Raj's thoughtful responses and supportive words had provided a new perspective on her feelings, helping her to navigate through the fog of uncertainty.

As Raina prepared to end her day, she reflected on the call with a sense of contentment. The first contact with Raj had been more than just a professional exchange—it had been a meaningful conversation that had touched on deeper aspects of her life. She felt a renewed sense of purpose and a glimmer of hope that the answers she sought might be closer than she had realized.

Raj, on the other hand, felt a sense of fulfillment from their conversation. It was clear that their connection was more than just academic; it was evolving into something more profound. As he wrapped up his work for the evening, he looked forward to their next conversation with a sense of anticipation, knowing that their journey together was only just beginning.

The cosmos had brought them together once more, and as they continued to explore their shared path, they were both eager to see where it would lead.

VII

The Urgent Meeting in Kharagpur

Raina's routine at IIT Kharagpur had settled into a familiar rhythm, with days consumed by research and nights filled with restless thoughts. Despite the lingering unease, she found solace in her work, diving deeper into her studies on photonic mass. The recent discussions with Raj had reinvigorated her, adding a fresh perspective to her research.

One afternoon, as Raina was in the midst of running simulations in her lab, she received an unexpected email from the department head. The subject line read: **"Urgent Meeting - Today at 4 PM."** Raina frowned. The suddenness of the meeting was unusual. Typically, meetings were scheduled well in advance, especially for something involving the entire department. She quickly checked with her colleagues, who were equally puzzled but had also received the same message.

As the clock approached 4 PM, Raina made her way to the conference room. The atmosphere was charged with anticipation and unease, as the other faculty members and researchers gathered, exchanging murmurs of speculation. What could be so urgent that it required an unscheduled meeting with the entire department?

The department head, Professor Menon, entered the room with a serious expression. The chatter died down immediately as everyone focused their attention on him. "Thank you all for coming on such short notice," Professor Menon began, his voice steady but carrying a weight of concern. "I'm afraid we have a situation that requires our immediate attention."

Raina exchanged a glance with Dr. Banerjee, who was sitting across the table. He raised an eyebrow, clearly as intrigued as she was.

Professor Menon continued, "We've received information from the Ministry of Science and Technology that there have been security breaches concerning sensitive research data across several servers, including our own. Given the nature of our work on photonic mass, we are considered a high-priority target."

A wave of shock rippled through the room. Raina's mind raced. The implications of such a breach were enormous, not just for their research but for national security. The work on photonic mass had far-reaching consequences, and any compromise of that data could have serious repercussions.

"We've been instructed to review all security protocols immediately," Professor Menon said. "This includes access to research labs, data encryption, and communication channels. Additionally, we need to ensure that our ongoing projects are secure and that any sensitive information is protected."

Raina felt a knot form in her stomach. The urgency in Professor Menon's tone made it clear that this was not a drill. The work she and her colleagues were doing was at the forefront of cutting-edge technology, and the thought of it being compromised sent a chill down her spine.

As the meeting progressed, detailed instructions were given on the steps each team needed to take. Raina listened carefully, already making mental notes of what needed to be done in her lab. She would have to double-check all the encryption methods, secure the physical access points, and possibly even restrict certain data to ensure its safety.

But amidst the technical details, Raina couldn't help but think of Raj. She wondered if his technology was implemented things would not have been like this. The urgency of the situation added another layer of complexity to their recent discussions.

As the meeting concluded, Raina felt a sense of determination settle over her. There was work to be done, and she couldn't afford to be distracted by her emotions or the unsettling sense of foreboding. The safety and integrity of their research were paramount, and she would do everything in her power to protect it.

The urgent meeting had just concluded, leaving the faculty and researchers at IIT Kharagpur in a state of heightened alert. Raina returned to her lab, her mind racing with the implications of the security breach. The gravity of the situation had been made clear—sensitive research data, including the groundbreaking work on photonic mass, was at risk. As she began reviewing the security protocols for her lab, Raina's thoughts kept circling back to Raj. Their recent conversations had touched on the importance of data integrity, but now those concerns seemed more pressing than ever. She couldn't shake the feeling that this breach might be connected to the broader implications of their work.

Just as she was about to start encrypting some of her most sensitive files, her phone buzzed with an incoming call. It was Professor Menon.

"Raina, I need you in the main conference room immediately," his voice was firm, leaving no room for delay. "We've brought in an expert from IIT Chennai to assist us with the security measures. I believe you'll want to be part of this discussion."

Curiosity piqued; Raina quickly made her way to the conference room. As she entered, she noticed a familiar figure standing by the projector—Raj. He looked up as she entered, and their eyes met, a flash of recognition passing between them. For a moment, the weight of the situation lifted, replaced by the simple pleasure of seeing a friend and colleague. But the seriousness of the meeting quickly brought them back to the matter at hand.

"Raina, this is Dr. Raj, an expert in photonic communication and data transfer technology from IIT Chennai," Professor Menon introduced, though Raina and Raj needed no introduction. "He's here to help us secure our systems and ensure that our research is protected."

Raj nodded in acknowledgment. "Given the nature of the breach and the sensitivity of your work, it's crucial that we implement the most advanced encryption and data transfer protocols. Photonic communication, with its potential for near-impenetrable security, is our best option." Raina felt a mixture of pride and concern as she listened to Raj speak. He was clearly the right person for the job, but the fact that he was here underscored just how serious the situation had become.

Over the next few hours, they communicated closely together, reviewing the existing security measures and discussing the implementation of photonic communication channels for data transfer. Raj's expertise was invaluable, and Raina found herself both learning from and collaborating with him in ways that deepened their professional bond.

As they wrapped up the session, Raj texted Raina aside. "I wanted to talk to you earlier, but I guess this situation expedited our meeting," he said with a hint of a smile. "How are you holding up?"

Raina appreciated the concern in his voice. "It's been overwhelming, but I'm managing. I'm just glad you're here to help us through this."

Raj nodded. "We'll get through it, Raina. Together."

The urgency of the day's events had brought them back into each other's orbit, not just as colleagues but as allies facing a common challenge. The security breach had revealed vulnerabilities not only in their work but also in the larger context of their field, pushing them to fortify their defenses and protect what they had worked so hard to achieve.

As Raina walked back to her lab, she couldn't help but feel a sense of reassurance. With Raj by her side, she knew they stood a better chance of weathering the storm ahead. The cosmos, it seemed, had conspired once again to bring them together, this time to protect something far greater than themselves. There was no time to waste. The urgency of the meeting had made it clear that they were dealing with a serious threat, and she needed to act quickly. But even as she busied herself with securing her research, a part of her mind lingered on Raj. She made a mental note to reach out to him later, to check if he was experiencing the same situation and to discuss how they could safeguard their collaborative work.

The following day Raj was in Kharagpur. The discussion they had shared had stirred a new sense of purpose within her. The unease she had been feeling now seemed to be channeling into her work with renewed vigor. The insights Raj had offered on the model reliability of the photonic mass were invaluable, and Raina found herself revisiting her research with fresh perspectives.

Yet, despite the professional satisfaction, Raina couldn't ignore the personal implications of their conversation. The way Raj had listened, the empathy in his voice—there was something comforting about it. It was as if he had offered her a lifeline, a bridge to understanding her own feelings and struggles. Meanwhile, Raj was equally engrossed in their conversation. He had spent hours reviewing their discussion and reflecting on the broader implications of their work. He appreciated Raina's analytical mind and the way she tackled complex problems. Their intellectual exchange had left him with a sense of anticipation for future collaborations.

It was late one evening when Raina's phone buzzed with a new message from Raj. She had been working late, her desk cluttered with papers and books, the glow of her laptop illuminating her focused expression. The message read:

"Hi Raina, I was thinking about our discussion and wanted to follow up. Are you free to meet tomorrow? I have a few more ideas I'd like to share."

Raina smiled as she read the message. It was a welcome distraction from her work. She quickly replied:

"Hi Raj, that sounds great. I'm available in the afternoon. Looking forward to it!"

The next day, Raina eagerly anticipated their conversation. The hours seemed to drag, her mind constantly drifting to the clock. As the appointed time drew near, she took a moment to prepare her notes, ready to dive back into their discussion on photonics.

When Raj came through, Raina answered with enthusiasm. "Hi Raj!"

"Hi Raina! I hope I'm not catching you at a bad time," Raj said, his voice carrying a familiar warmth.

"Not at all. I'm glad to hear from you. What's on your mind?"

Raj took a deep breath. "I've been thinking about the implications of our work and how it intersects with some emerging theories in photonics. I've come across some recent papers that might shed light on the areas we discussed."

As they delved into the technical details, Raina felt a renewed sense of excitement. The conversation flowed effortlessly, with both of them contributing ideas and exploring new angles. It was a dynamic exchange, filled with the kind of intellectual synergy that both had missed since their last encounter.

After they had wrapped up their discussion, Raj hesitated for a moment. "Raina, there's something else I've been meaning to ask. How have you been feeling? You mentioned some unease in our last call."

Raina paused, her thoughts turning to the personal struggles she had been facing. "It's still there. I've been trying to understand it better. I think talking with you has helped a lot, though. It's like you've given me a new perspective."

"I'm glad to hear that," Raj said gently. "Sometimes, just having someone to talk to can make a big difference. And if you ever need to share more, I'm here."

Raina felt a wave of relief wash over her. It was comforting to know that Raj was genuinely concerned, not just about their work but also about her well-being.

"Thank you, Raj. I really appreciate that," Raina replied. "It means a lot to me."

As she returned to her work, Raina felt a shift within her. The pain and unease that had been lingering seemed to have found a new outlet. The first contact with Raj had marked the beginning of a new chapter where professional collaboration and personal connection intertwined, leading her toward a deeper understanding of herself and her work.

The urgent meeting in Kharagpur had not only heightened Raina's awareness of the vulnerabilities in their field but also deepened her resolve. The path ahead was fraught with challenges, but she knew that she and Raj would face them together, navigating the uncertainties that lay ahead with a shared sense of purpose and determination.

After the urgent meeting in Kharagpur, Raina found herself increasingly drawn into the investigation. The research suspension was frustrating, but it gave her time to focus on understanding the breach and how to prevent it from happening again. She remained in close contact with Raj, sharing updates and brainstorming possible solutions.

Next evening, Raj called her with an idea. "Raina, I've been thinking about how we can secure our data better. There's a technology I've been developing—a sophisticated encryption system tailored specifically for photonic communication. It's designed to detect and counteract unauthorized access by analyzing patterns in data transmission. I believe it could help us identify the source of the breach."

Raina was intrigued. "That sounds promising, Raj. If it works, it could not only secure our data but also trace back to whoever is responsible."

Raj wasted no time. He worked tirelessly to implement the technology in Raina's lab, coordinating with the IT team at IIT Kharagpur to ensure it was integrated seamlessly into their existing systems. The process was meticulous, but within days, the new security measures were in place.

The impact was immediate. The system began to detect irregularities in the data transmissions, flagging suspicious activities that had previously gone unnoticed. Raj's technology not only secured the research data but also provided crucial information that helped the investigators trace the breach. Days later, Raina received a call from Dr. Menon, the department director. His voice was filled with a mix of relief and urgency. "Raina, we've identified the source of the breach. It's a Chinese research firm that's been working in the same field of photonic communication as us. They were attempting to steal our data to advance their own research." This firm had been aggressively pursuing advancements in the same area and had resorted to unethical means to obtain critical data from Raina's team

Raina's heart sank as she absorbed the gravity of the situation. The theft was not just a random act of cybercrime; it was part of a larger, more calculated effort to undermine their work.

Dr. Menon continued, "Thanks to Raj's technology, we were able to detect and trace the breach. The authorities have been informed, and they're taking the necessary steps to address this on an international level. Your collaboration with Raj was instrumental in resolving this crisis."

Raina felt a surge of pride and gratitude. "I'm just glad we could help. This was a team effort, and Raj's expertise was crucial."

After the call, Raina reached out to Raj to share the news. "Raj, your technology worked! We've identified the culprits—it was a Chinese research firm trying to steal our data."

Raj sighed with relief. "I'm glad we could stop them, Raina. It's a reminder of how critical our work is and how important it is to protect it."

Raina nodded, even though he couldn't see her. "Absolutely. I'm just grateful that we were able to prevent any further damage."

With the implementation of Raj's cutting-edge technology, the issue of the security breach was swiftly addressed. The sophisticated measures Raj had proposed and helped implement strengthened the security protocols, allowing the research team to trace the origins of the unauthorized access.

The discovery sent shockwaves through the academic and scientific community. It became clear that the competition in the field of photonic communication was not just about who could achieve the next breakthrough, but also about protecting intellectual property and ensuring that research efforts remained secure.

Raina and her colleagues felt a mix of relief and anger. The relief came from knowing that the breach had been detected and the threat neutralized. The anger stemmed from the realization that their hard work had been targeted by a rival organization willing to cross ethical boundaries.

Raj, who had been closely involved in resolving the issue, felt a deep sense of responsibility. His technology had not only prevented further data theft but also exposed the culprits. He knew that this was just the beginning of a larger conversation about international cooperation and competition in advanced scientific fields.

As Raina and Raj discussed the situation, they both agreed that the experience had brought them closer as colleagues and friends. They had faced a significant challenge together and had emerged stronger, both in their professional capabilities and in their understanding of the complex world of scientific research. The incident also served as a wake-up call for the entire research community. It highlighted the need for enhanced collaboration, not just within a country but across borders, to protect scientific progress and ensure that innovation was driven by mutual respect and shared goals, rather than by rivalry and theft.

The resolution of the crisis brought a sense of closure to the chaotic events of the past few weeks. With the breach detected and the security measures in place, Raina's team was able to resume their research. The collaboration with Raj had not only strengthened their professional bond but also highlighted the importance of trust and innovation in the face of adversity.

As Raina returned to her work, she knew that the challenges ahead would be different, but she was better prepared to face them. The experience had taught her valuable lessons about resilience, the power of collaboration, and the necessity of protecting the knowledge that had the potential to change the world.

VIII

The Communication Within

Raina sat in her dimly lit apartment in Kharagpur, the weight of recent events pressing down on her. The silence of the night was punctuated only by the soft hum of her laptop, which lay open on the desk before her. The evening light casting long shadows on the walls. She had always been someone who thrived on structure, on clear goals and objectives, but lately, things had started to unravel. The unease she felt had grown into something more—a constant dialogue within her mind that she could no longer ignore. The events of the past few weeks had left her feeling isolated and introspective. Despite the breakthroughs in their work and the resolution of the security breach, there was a lingering sense of unease within her. It was as if the answers she sought were just out of reach, obscured by a fog of uncertainty. In moments like these, Raina found herself talking to herself more often. She had vocalized her thoughts, trying to untangle the web of emotions and ideas swirling in her mind. It was a coping mechanism, a way to bring clarity to her internal chaos.

The other evening, as she sat at her desk, she decided to write down her thoughts. The act of writing felt more concrete, more deliberate. She opened her notebook and began to jot down the random musings that had been occupying her mind. Raina sat at her desk, her fingers hovering over the keyboard, struggling to capture the whirlwind of thoughts that had been consuming her mind. The recent events—the security breach, the revelations about the Chinese research firm, her deepening conversations with Raj—had left her in a state of introspection she hadn't experienced before. She found herself talking to herself more often, trying to make sense of the emotions swirling within her. As she stared at the blinking cursor on her screen, she decided to do something she hadn't done in a long time: write down her thoughts, not as part of her research, but as a way to process what was happening inside her. She began typing, letting the words flow without restraint.

*Raj, I've started talking to myself a lot lately. Maybe it's because there's so much going on inside my head that I need to sort out. Sometimes, the only way to make sense of it all is to hear it out loud. Do you ever feel like that? *

*I've been thinking about our conversation on the photonic mass model. The way you explained the nuances made everything click for me. It's fascinating how a fresh perspective can open up new avenues of thought. I wonder if there's a way to apply this to our everyday lives—seeing things from different angles to find clarity. *

*Since the breach, I've felt a mix of relief and anxiety. We caught the culprits, but it made me realize how vulnerable our work can be. It's not just about science anymore; it's about protecting it, nurturing it. How do you cope with that kind of pressure? *

*I've been having these dreams lately. They're vivid and unsettling, almost as if they're trying to tell me something. In one dream, I'm standing on the edge of a cliff, looking out at a vast, empty space. It feels both freeing and terrifying. Do you ever have dreams like that? *

Raina paused, looking at the words she had written. There was a certain catharsis in seeing her thoughts laid out before her. She realized that sharing these with Raj might help her find the clarity she sought. With a determined nod, she typed up her notes and sent them off in an email to Raj.

She leaned back in her chair, closing her eyes, and let the thoughts flow freely.

"Raj, I'm making random thoughts about you," she whispered into the stillness. "It's like my mind has created this separate version of you, someone who is always there, always listening, even when you're not. I talk to this version of you in my head, asking questions, seeking answers, trying to make sense of everything that's happening."

Raina reached for her journal, flipping it open to a blank page. She began to write, her hand moving almost mechanically as the words poured out.

*"Dear Raj, I don't know when it started, but I find myself having these conversations with you in my mind. They're not like the ones we've had over the phone or during our meetings. These are different. They're raw, unfiltered. It's like I'm talking to a part of myself that you somehow represent. Maybe it's because you've been the one person

who's understood me in a way that no one else has, or maybe it's because I trust you to see the parts of me that I can't show to others.*"

"Sometimes, these thoughts are comforting. I imagine you giving me advice, helping me untangle the mess in my head. Other times, they're overwhelming, as if I'm caught in a loop that I can't escape. I want to share these thoughts with you, to let you see the side of me that's struggling to keep it all together. But I'm afraid. Afraid that you'll see me as weak, or worse, that you'll feel the same way and we'll both be lost in this uncertainty."*

She paused, staring at the words on the page. They felt like a confession, a glimpse into the part of her that was too vulnerable to reveal in the light of day. Yet, she couldn't stop writing.

"I think about what you might say if you knew. Would you understand? Would you tell me that it's okay, that everyone goes through moments like this? Or would you be concerned, worried that I'm losing my grip on reality?"

"I'm not sure what's happening to me, Raj. I used to be so sure of myself, so confident in my path. But now, everything feels uncertain. It's as if the ground beneath my feet is shifting, and I'm struggling to find my balance. I keep wondering if you feel the same way. Do you have moments when everything seems too much? When you're not sure if you're making the right choices?"

"I wish I could hear your thoughts, the ones you don't share with anyone else. Maybe then, I wouldn't feel so alone in this."

Raina set the pen down, closing her journal with a heavy sigh. The act of writing had been cathartic, a release of the thoughts that had been swirling in her mind for days. But it also left her feeling exposed, as if she had laid bare her soul on the page.

Still, she couldn't shake the feeling that Raj would understand, that he might even welcome her honesty. After all, he had always been the one to encourage her to speak her mind, to share her thoughts without fear of judgment.

Taking a deep breath, Raina picked up her phone and typed a message to Raj:

"Raj, I've been having these thoughts, these conversations with you in my mind. I started writing them down. If you're okay with it, I'd like to share them with you. Maybe you could do the same? It might help us both to get through this."

Raj, I don't know if I'm writing this to you or to myself. Maybe both. Lately, I've found myself talking to myself, as if trying to have a conversation that no one else can hear or understand. I think it's because there are so many things I can't quite articulate aloud—thoughts that don't make sense yet, feelings that are too complex to voice. But I need to get them out, so here I am, writing them down.

I've started making random thoughts about you, Raj. I wonder if you've noticed the same about me. I imagine you do the same—talk to yourself, I mean. We're both thinkers, after all, always lost in our heads. I guess that's why I feel this strange connection with you. It's not just about the work, though that's part of it. It's something deeper, something I can't fully explain.

I keep thinking about our conversations, how you listen to me so thoughtfully, how you seem to understand things I haven't even said. It's rare to find someone who can do that. I feel like you're not just hearing my words but the spaces between them, the unsaid parts that even I don't fully understand.

Sometimes, I catch myself wondering what you're thinking when we're not talking. Do you ever think about me, the way I think about you? I know that sounds odd, maybe even a little too personal, but it's the truth. I've been trying to make sense of this—whatever this is between us—and the more I think about it, the more it feels like something important, something that matters.

I want to start sharing these thoughts with you, Raj, but I'm not sure how. Maybe it's too soon, or maybe I'm just afraid of what it might mean. But I think I'll start writing them down, just like this, and when the time feels right, I'll send them to you. Maybe you'll understand, or maybe you won't, but I need to do this, if only for myself.

I've always believed that every relationship has an expiry date, but I wonder if that's true. Maybe some connections are meant to last longer, or maybe they leave an imprint on us that never really fades, even if the relationship itself does. I don't know where this is going, Raj, or what it means, but I want to find out. And I want you to be a part of that journey with me.

Raina paused, reading over what she had just written. Her heart pounded in her chest, a mix of fear and relief washing over her. She didn't know if she would ever have the courage to send these words to Raj, but for now, it felt good to let them out. To give voice to the thoughts that had been building inside her, even if only in written form.

She saved the document and closed her laptop, feeling a strange sense of calm. For now, these words would remain hers alone, but the possibility of sharing them with Raj one day lingered in the back of her mind.

This exchange marked a new phase in their relationship. It was no longer just about professional collaboration; it was about understanding and supporting each other through the complexities of life and work. As they continued to share their thoughts, they found solace and strength in their connection, realizing that sometimes, talking to oneself can be the first step in truly communicating with another.

She hesitated for a moment before hitting send, her heart pounding in her chest. There was no turning back now.

IX

All Are My Thoughts, and I Will Keep Them Always with Me

As Raina used to sit alone in her dimly lit apartment, her mind racing with thoughts that seemed to swirl endlessly. The quiet hum of the ceiling fan and the distant sounds of the city outside barely registered as she delved deeper into her reflections. The past few months had been a whirlwind of emotions, discoveries, and connections—each one leaving an indelible mark on her psyche.

As she gazed at the scattered papers on her desk, remnants of her ongoing research, Raina realized that the most profound changes in her life were not in the equations she solved or the experiments she conducted, but in the thoughts that had taken root in her mind. These thoughts, born from her interactions with Raj, the recent challenges at work, and her own internal struggles, had become an integral part of her.

She knew that these thoughts, both comforting and unsettling, were hers alone. They were the essence of her experiences, the silent witnesses to her journey. No one else could fully understand them, and she was okay with that. They were a reflection of who she was, of the person she had become through her trials and triumphs.

Raina's thoughts were not just fleeting ideas or passing emotions. They were her companions, guiding her through moments of doubt and clarity, through loneliness and connection. She had poured over them, dissected them, and tried to make sense of them. And now, as she sat in the stillness of her room, she realized how precious they were to her.

She thought of Raj and the impact he had made on her life. Their conversations, both profound and mundane, had stirred something deep within her. He had helped her see the world from a different perspective, challenging her ideas and pushing her to think beyond the confines of her work. But more than that, he had made her confront her own emotions, her own insecurities, and the complexities of human connection.

These were the thoughts she would carry with her, long after the memories of their meetings and phone calls had faded. They were the thoughts that would stay with her, shaping her decisions and guiding her through whatever came next.

Raina picked up her notebook, the one she had kept since she started her post-doc in Kharagpur. It was filled with scribbles, equations, and notes from seminars. But in between the technical jargon, there were pages where she had poured out her heart—where she had written down the thoughts that plagued her during sleepless nights, the ones that brought her solace in times of distress.

As she flipped through the pages, she felt a sense of ownership over these thoughts. They were hers, and she would keep them with her always. They were the record of her journey, the proof of her growth, and the foundation of her future.

Raina knew that life would continue to challenge her, to present her with situations that would test her resolve and force her to adapt. But she also knew that she had a reservoir of strength within her, built from the thoughts she had nurtured and the experiences she had endured.

These thoughts were not just memories—they were lessons, reminders of what she had been through and what she had overcome. They were the silent companions that would walk with her through the days to come, offering comfort in times of need and clarity in moments of confusion.

Raina closed the notebook and placed it gently on her desk. She took a deep breath, feeling a sense of calm wash over her. The world outside was chaotic and unpredictable, but within her, there was a sanctuary of thoughts that she could always return to.

No matter where life took her, no matter what challenges lay ahead, Raina knew that she would carry these thoughts with her. They were her most treasured possessions, the essence of her being, and she would keep them close, always.

With that realization, Raina felt a renewed sense of purpose. She wasn't just a scientist or a researcher; she was a thinker, a dreamer, a woman who had embraced the complexities of her own mind. And in that embrace, she found strength, resilience, and a quiet, unshakable peace.

X

You are My Thought and I Will Keep you Always With Me

Raina sat in her favorite corner of the café in Kharagpur, a steaming cup of coffee in front of her. The sun was setting, casting a warm, golden glow through the large windows. The café was bustling with the usual evening crowd, but Raina's mind was miles away.

Her thoughts drifted to the whirlwind of events that had recently unfolded—the security breach, the intense work to resolve it, and her conversations with Raj. Each moment, each experience, had left an indelible mark on her psyche. As she sipped her coffee, she realized how deeply these thoughts and feelings had become a part of her.

Despite the challenges and uncertainties, Raina found herself cherishing the introspective journey she had been on. She had always been someone who valued her thoughts, her reflections, and the quiet moments of understanding that came with them. Now, more than ever, she felt a profound connection to the inner world she had built.

She pulled out her notebook, a trusted companion over the years, and began to write. Her pen moved fluidly across the pages, capturing fragments of her thoughts, memories, and emotions.

"Every challenge we face shapes us in ways we often don't realize at the moment. The breach, the stress, the long conversations with Raj—they have all been catalysts for deeper introspection. I am not just my achievements or my failures; I am the sum of all my experiences, thoughts, and feelings. And these, I will keep with me, always."

Raina paused, looking at the words she had just written. They felt true and resonant. She realized that it wasn't just the events themselves that mattered, but how she perceived and internalized them. Her thoughts were a sanctuary, a place where she could find clarity and peace amidst the chaos of the external world.

She thought about Raj and their growing connection. Their conversations had been a source of comfort and inspiration, a reminder that she wasn't alone in her journey. Yet, she also understood that the bond they shared was just one part of a much larger tapestry of her life.

"Relationships, like everything else, come and go. But the impact they leave, the thoughts they inspire, those remain with us forever. Raj has been a significant part of my recent journey, but even if our paths diverge, the insights and growth I've gained will stay with me."

Raina felt a sense of gratitude wash over her. For the experiences, for the people who had touched her life, and for the strength she had found within herself. She knew that the future was uncertain, but she was at peace with that uncertainty. Her thoughts and reflections had become a source of strength and resilience.

As she continued to write, Raina felt a deep sense of connection to herself. She realized that no matter what happened, she would always have her thoughts, her reflections, and the wisdom she had gained along the way. They were her constant companions, her inner compass guiding her through the ebb and flow of life.

"All are my thoughts," she wrote, "and I will keep them always with me. They are the essence of who I am, the silent narrators of my journey. Through them, I find meaning, purpose, and a sense of self that transcends the transient nature of the world around me."

Raina closed her notebook and took another sip of her coffee, feeling a profound sense of contentment. She knew that whatever challenges lay ahead, she was ready to face them with grace and courage. Her thoughts were her treasure, her refuge, and her guide. And as long as she had them, she knew she would never be lost.

Raina sat alone in her office, the soft hum of the air conditioner the only sound accompanying her thoughts. The evening sun cast long shadows across her desk, where papers and research notes lay scattered. Despite the quiet surroundings, her mind was anything but still.

Over the past few months, Raina had been on a tumultuous journey—both professionally and personally. The challenges with her research, the unsettling security breach, the reconnection with Raj, and the complex emotions that had surfaced all swirled in her mind like a storm. Yet, through it all, one thing had remained constant: her thoughts.

These thoughts were her companions, her confidants, the silent witnesses to her struggles and triumphs. They had been with her through sleepless nights, long hours in the lab, and moments of doubt and fear. They had guided her when the path was unclear and comforted her when she felt alone.

Raina knew that these thoughts were more than just fleeting moments of reflection. They were a part of her—intimate, personal, and deeply meaningful. Each one represented a piece of her journey, a fragment of the experiences that had shaped her. And as much as she had shared with Raj and others, there were thoughts that she kept to herself, private and precious.

Sitting at her desk, Raina allowed herself to delve into these thoughts, letting them wash over her like a soothing wave. She thought about the first time she had met Raj in Chennai, the way their professional relationship had blossomed into something more profound. She remembered the conversations they had shared, the laughter, the tension, the unspoken understanding that had grown between them.

She thought about the moments of doubt she had faced—when the security breach threatened everything she had worked for, when the weight of her responsibilities felt overwhelming, and when she questioned whether she was on the right path. These thoughts had often been her only solace, helping her navigate the complexities of her world.

Raina realized that these thoughts were hers alone, a treasure trove of memories, reflections, and emotions that she could carry with her wherever she went. No matter what happened in the future—whether her relationship with Raj faded, whether her research took an unexpected turn, or whether life led her down a completely different path—these thoughts would always be with her, a constant source of strength and wisdom.

In this quiet moment of introspection, Raina made a promise to herself. She would keep these thoughts close, nurture them, and draw from them whenever she needed guidance or reassurance. They were a part of her identity, a testament to her resilience and growth. And no matter how the world around her changed, these thoughts would remain, a sanctuary within her mind.

Raina took a deep breath, feeling a sense of peace settle over her. She knew that she didn't have all the answers, and that life would continue to throw challenges her way. But she also knew that she had everything she needed within her—her thoughts, her experiences, her inner strength. These were the things that no one could take away from her, the things that would guide her through whatever lay ahead.

As the sun dipped below the horizon, Raina stood up from her desk, feeling lighter, more centered. She looked out at the darkening sky, a small smile playing on her lips. The world outside was vast and unpredictable, but inside, within her thoughts, she had found a place of calm and certainty.

"All are my thoughts," she whispered to herself, "and I will keep them always with me."

With that, she turned off the lights in her office, gathered her belongings, and stepped out into the cool evening air. The future awaited her, full of possibilities and unknowns. But whatever came her way, Raina knew she would be ready, carrying her thoughts with her, always.

Raina sat at her writing desk, surrounded by a sea of notebooks and loose sheets of paper. The once vibrant and orderly workspace now resembled a chaotic mosaic of her mind—a reflection of the thoughts and emotions she had been grappling with for what felt like an eternity.

For days, she had been diligently penning down her reflections, ideas, and musings. What had started as a means to make sense of her turbulent emotions had gradually become an overwhelming collection of fragmented thoughts. As she looked around at the disarray, a sense of frustration began to take hold.

Each page contained a different piece of her mind: questions without answers, observations that seemed to lead nowhere, and epiphanies that quickly faded into the background of her busy life. It was as if her thoughts were both a treasure trove and a burden, filled with potential but lacking direction.

Raina sighed deeply, her gaze falling on a particularly scribbled-on sheet. The words on it seemed to echo her current sentiment: *"I feel lost in the sea of my own thoughts. They come and go, but what am I supposed to do with them?"* She had hoped that by writing them down, she would find clarity, but instead, she felt more entangled in her own mental labyrinth.

She picked up one of the notebooks, flipping through pages filled with her handwriting. Some thoughts were profound, others mundane. There were ideas about her research, reflections on her interactions with Raj, and scattered personal insights. Yet, despite the volume of material, she felt no closer to understanding what to do with it all.

Raina thought about her earlier conversations with Raj and their discussions about the nature of their work. She had always admired his ability to see patterns and connections where others saw chaos. Perhaps it was time to approach her own thoughts with a similar mindset.

Taking a deep breath, Raina decided to sort through the mess. She pulled out a clean notebook and began organizing her scattered pages into themes: professional insights, personal reflections, and unresolved questions. As she did this, she started to see connections between her thoughts that she hadn't noticed before.

Some of the ideas were related to her research, others to her personal growth, and a few were about the nature of relationships and connections. By categorizing them, Raina was beginning to make sense of the seemingly random pieces of her mental puzzle.

With renewed focus, she began to jot down potential ways to integrate her thoughts into her work and personal life. She considered setting aside dedicated time to explore her ideas further, perhaps turning some of her reflections into a structured project or paper.

Raina also recognized the importance of sharing her thoughts with others. It wasn't just about writing them down; it was about discussing them, seeking feedback, and finding ways to make them actionable. She decided to reach out to Raj, not just for professional collaboration but also for his perspective on her personal reflections.

As the days went on, Raina continued to refine her approach. She began to see her random thoughts not as a burden but as a source of inspiration. The process of organizing and reflecting on them helped her gain a clearer understanding of her own mind and its various facets.

Ultimately, Raina realized that the value of her thoughts lay not in having them perfectly ordered or fully resolved but in the act of engaging with them. By embracing the randomness and finding ways to channel her insights, she was able to create a meaningful path forward.

One evening, as she looked at her neatly organized notebooks and the new ideas that had emerged from her reflections, Raina felt a sense of accomplishment. She had taken her scattered thoughts and transformed them into something tangible, something that could guide her future endeavors.

With a sense of contentment, she closed her notebook and turned off the desk lamp. It had been a journey of sorting through chaos to find clarity, and she had come out of it with a deeper appreciation for the complexity of her own mind.

As she stepped away from her desk, Raina felt a renewed sense of purpose. Her thoughts, once a jumble of randomness, had found a place within her life. And with that, she was ready to move forward, carrying with her the lessons learned from the intricate dance of her own reflections.

Raina stared at the stack of notebooks piled on her desk, each one filled with her handwritten musings, reflections, and random thoughts. The once neatly organized pages now seemed like a chaotic collection of ideas and observations. It had been weeks since she had started this practice, and the initial excitement of pouring her thoughts onto paper had given way to a sense of confusion.

Each notebook contained fragments of her inner world—some profound, others trivial, but all deeply personal. She had been writing feverishly, trying to make sense of the swirling thoughts in her mind. The act of writing had been cathartic, a way to process her experiences and emotions. But now, as she looked at the collection, she felt overwhelmed by the sheer volume of her reflections.

Raina flipped through the pages, reading snippets of her own words. There were notes about her research, observations about her interactions with Raj, and musings on the nature of relationships and the passage of time. Some pages were filled with questions she had yet to answer, while others captured fleeting insights that seemed significant at the moment but now felt fragmented and disjointed.

She wondered what to do with all these random thoughts. Should she try to organize them, to find some pattern or theme? Or should she let them remain as they were—unstructured and free-form? The question gnawed at her, adding to the sense of uncertainty she had been feeling.

Raina sighed and leaned back in her chair. She had always been someone who sought order and clarity, whether in her research or her personal life. The chaotic nature of her notebooks seemed at odds with her desire for precision and purpose. Yet, there was something undeniably valuable in these scattered reflections—perhaps in their very randomness lay the essence of her journey.

As she pondered, Raina recalled a conversation she had had with Raj about the nature of creativity and inspiration. He had mentioned that sometimes, the most profound ideas emerged from seemingly random thoughts and experiences. It wasn't about forcing order but rather about allowing the thoughts to reveal their significance over time.

With this in mind, Raina decided to approach her notebooks with a different perspective. Instead of trying to impose structure on them, she would allow herself to explore the connections between her thoughts. Perhaps there was a larger narrative emerging from the chaos, one that she could only see by stepping back and observing the patterns that naturally formed.

She began to select passages from her notebooks that resonated with her the most. As she read through them, she started to notice recurring themes and ideas—concepts about relationships, personal growth, and the interplay between professional and personal life. It was as if the random thoughts were piecing together a mosaic, revealing insights she hadn't fully grasped before.

Raina decided to create a new project from these reflections—a collection of essays or a personal journal that would capture her evolving understanding of the topics she had explored. She would approach it not as an attempt to impose order but as an opportunity to embrace the spontaneity of her thoughts and see where they led her.

With renewed purpose, Raina began organizing her notes into broad categories, not to confine them but to highlight the threads that connected them. She allowed herself to be flexible and open-minded, letting the process of discovery guide her. The notebooks, once a source of confusion, now became a source of inspiration and potential.

As she worked on this new project, Raina felt a sense of liberation. The random thoughts that had once seemed overwhelming were now taking shape, revealing a tapestry of her inner world. It wasn't about finding definitive answers but about exploring the journey of her thoughts and embracing the beauty of their randomness.

Raina closed her latest notebook with a satisfied smile. She had discovered that there was value in embracing the unpredictability of her thoughts, in allowing them to guide her rather than trying to control them. In doing so, she had found a new way to engage with her own mind—a way that honored both the order she sought and the chaos she had embraced.

With this newfound understanding, Raina felt ready to continue her journey, knowing that her thoughts were not just random musings but integral pieces of her story.

Raj had been spending long hours at the campus, deeply engrossed in the new development of the Photonic Mass Interface. The project had gained significant momentum, and Raj, along with his team, was on the verge of a breakthrough. His thoughts were consumed with calculations, models, and experimental data, leaving little room for anything else. Yet, despite the intensity of his work, Raina had been on his mind more than he cared to admit.

On this particular afternoon, Raina found herself walking towards Raj's office. The notebook in her hands was filled with scribbles, equations, and personal reflections—things she had been working on in quiet moments when she wasn't immersed in her own research. But this time, it wasn't just about work. There was something more she needed to share with him.

When she reached the door, she hesitated for a moment before knocking softly. Raj looked up from his desk, surprised but pleased to see her. His eyes briefly shifted from the glowing equations on his computer screen to the notebook she was clutching tightly.

"Raina, come in," he said, pushing aside a stack of papers to make room for her.

She stepped inside, feeling a mix of anticipation and nervousness. There had been so many moments in their previous interactions where she had wanted to express what was on her mind, but the timing had never seemed right. Today, though, felt different.

"I've been thinking," Raina began, carefully choosing her words. "About everything that's happened—between us, the work we've been doing, and... other things."

Raj leaned forward, his expression softening. "What's on your mind?"

She handed him the notebook. "I've written some thoughts down. Some of it is about the project, but most of it... it's personal. I've been trying to make sense of what I've been feeling."

Raj opened the notebook slowly, his fingers tracing the edges of the pages. As he began reading, the silence in the room grew thick with unspoken emotions. The first few pages were familiar—mathematical models, notes on the Photonic Mass Interface—but as he read on, he saw a shift. The equations faded into reflections, musings about life, and emotions that had been swirling within Raina for months.

She watched him carefully, her heart racing as he read her words. She had poured herself into that notebook, and now, sharing it with Raj felt like exposing a piece of her soul.

"I've been feeling a lot of things since we reconnected," Raina continued, her voice barely above a whisper. "I didn't know how to say it, so I wrote it down. This is what I've been holding back."

Raj set the notebook down gently, his gaze meeting hers. There was a quiet understanding in his eyes, as though he had been waiting for this moment too.

"Raina," he began slowly, "I've sensed that something's been weighing on you. I didn't want to push, but I knew there was more than just the work."

She nodded, feeling a lump in her throat. "It's been confusing, Raj. The connection we have, it's not just professional. And I don't know where that leaves us."

For a long moment, neither of them spoke. The weight of what had just been shared hung in the air between them, raw and real.

Raj finally stood up, walking over to where Raina sat. He knelt beside her, reaching for her hand. "Whatever happens next, we'll face it together," he said softly. "But I want you to know that your thoughts, your feelings—they matter. We don't have to rush to figure everything out."

Raina felt a surge of relief wash over her. In that moment, it wasn't about defining what they were or where they were headed. It was simply about being seen, heard, and understood. And that, for now, was enough.

Together, they sat in the quiet of the office, with the notebook lying open on the table between them—an unspoken promise that their connection, though indeterminate, was real and evolving.

XI

Photonic Mass Interface

Raj's words lingered in the air, heavy with the tension of unspoken realities.

"I am with you, Raina," he said softly, his hand still resting on hers. "But you know about the Photonic Mass Interface... and the Chinese connection to it."

Raina's heart skipped a beat. She knew this was coming, yet hearing him say it out loud made the situation feel even more precarious. The Photonic Mass Interface wasn't just an academic breakthrough anymore—it had taken on geopolitical significance. The breach they had uncovered, tied to a Chinese research firm working in the same field, had elevated their project to something far more complex and dangerous.

"I know," Raina whispered, pulling her hand back slightly, her mind already racing. "I've been thinking about it ever since we detected the theft. This isn't just about our research anymore, is it?"

Raj shook his head, his face somber. "No, it's not. The advancements we're making... they're critical, not just for scientific progress, but for national security. The implications are enormous. The fact that they've been trying to access our work means there's something at stake that goes beyond academic curiosity."

Raina felt the weight of his words settle on her shoulders. She had always viewed her work through the lens of intellectual curiosity and innovation. But now, standing on the brink of something much larger, she realized that the stakes had changed. The Chinese connection wasn't just a distant concern; it was a direct threat to the integrity of their research and the safety of the technology they were developing.

"I didn't want to involve you in this," Raj continued, his voice steady but tinged with concern. "But you're already part of it, whether we like it or not. The Photonic Mass Interface is too valuable. We have to be careful—every move we make, every conversation we have, could be monitored or intercepted."

Raina nodded, her mind flashing back to the subtle unease she had felt since returning to Kharagpur. The strange sense of being watched, the subtle nudges in her thoughts, it all started to make sense now. She wasn't just imagining things; there was a real danger lurking behind their work.

"What do we do?" she asked, her voice barely above a whisper.

Raj leaned closer, his eyes locked on hers. "We stay vigilant. We protect our research, and we make sure it doesn't fall into the wrong hands. But more than that, we have to trust each other. We're in this together, Raina. Whatever happens next, we'll face it side by side."

Raina took a deep breath, feeling a mix of fear and determination rise within her. The road ahead was uncertain, filled with potential risks and dangers she hadn't anticipated. But with Raj by her side, she knew they could navigate it together.

For the first time in weeks, despite the looming threats, Raina felt a sense of clarity. The challenges ahead were daunting, but she wasn't alone. Raj's steady presence, his unwavering support, gave her the strength to face whatever lay ahead.

"We'll be careful," she said firmly. "We'll protect what we've built. And we'll make sure it doesn't fall into the wrong hands."

Raj nodded, his expression resolute. "Exactly. We'll take this one step at a time. But for now, we need to focus on the next phase of the project. The world is watching, and we can't afford to slip."

As they sat there, the quiet hum of the campus around them, Raina felt a renewed sense of purpose. The journey ahead wouldn't be easy, but with Raj's partnership and the strength of their shared determination, she knew they would face whatever challenges the Photonic Mass Interface—and its shadowy connections—threw their way.

XII

I am with you Raj

Raina sat in her office, her mind racing with possibilities. The weight of everything—the project, the Chinese connection, and her own personal journey—pressed heavily on her, but there was one thing she had decided: she was ready to devote herself fully to the Photonic Mass Interface. For her, this wasn't just about technological advancement or securing the future of national security. It had become something more profound. Raina wanted to use this breakthrough to change everything—the past, the future, and even time itself.

The idea had been swirling in her mind for months now. Ever since she had delved into the deeper potential of photonics, Raina had begun to believe in the possibility of bending the fabric of time and space. She had read theories about parallel universes and alternate timelines, about how the smallest change in the past could ripple forward to create a completely new future. And now, she was starting to believe that their work on the Photonic Mass Interface could unlock the key to making that paradox a reality.

As she stared at her research notes, her thoughts went deeper. She wasn't just trying to create a technological breakthrough; she was trying to reshape the flow of time itself. If they succeeded, they could open up the possibility of creating a parallel universe—a place where choices didn't have to lead to the same outcomes, where the past could be altered to bring about a different future.

Raina's reasons were intensely personal. She had spent years haunted by the choices she had made, by the paths she had taken that had led her to this moment. There were things she wished she could undo, moments in time that had shifted her life in ways she hadn't anticipated. But what if she could go back and change those moments? What if, with this technology, she could create a new timeline, one where the mistakes of the past didn't have to define the future?

As she thought about it, her heart raced with both excitement and fear. The concept of altering the timeline was dangerous, uncharted territory. But it also held the potential for something extraordinary.

"I can't change the past," she whispered to herself, "but maybe I can change the consequences."

Raina knew that if she was going to pursue this path, it would mean diving even deeper into the heart of the Photonic Mass Interface. The theoretical models they had been working on could potentially create a framework that would allow them to manipulate time on a quantum level. It was audacious, even bordering on impossible, but she had always believed that the greatest breakthroughs came from pushing the boundaries of what people believed to be achievable.

In her mind, this wasn't just about bending time—it was about creating a new world, a parallel universe that could coexist alongside the one she lived in. A place where different choices led to different outcomes. A place where the future wasn't set in stone but was as malleable as the present.

But there was a cost. Raina knew that if she went down this path, she would have to give herself completely to the project. It would consume her—her time, her energy, her very essence. The connections she had with the people around her, including Raj, would be tested in ways she couldn't predict. But she was ready to take that risk. She was ready to sacrifice what she had for the chance to change what could be.

In her heart, Raina was driven by a single, unwavering belief: that the past did not have to define the future. And with the Photonic Mass Interface, she believed she had the key to unlocking that truth.

She leaned back in her chair, feeling a surge of determination wash over her. The path ahead was uncertain, and the risks were enormous. But she had made her choice.

She would devote herself to this technology, not just to advance science or to protect national security, but to reshape the very fabric of time itself. To create a future where the past didn't hold her captive, where she could rewrite the rules of the universe.

A future where everything could be different. A future she would create.

Raina was ready to devote herself entirely to the development of the Photonic Mass Interface. The project had evolved beyond a mere academic pursuit; it was now intertwined with her deepest desires and aspirations. She had a vision—one that stretched beyond the confines of their present reality. Raina wanted to change the past, to alter the future, and create a parallel universe paradox. This wasn't just about technological advancement; it was about reshaping existence itself.

As she sat in her lab that night, surrounded by glowing screens and the hum of high-tech equipment, Raina felt a surge of determination. She had spent years studying the intricacies of photonics and the mathematical models that could make her vision a reality. The Photonic Mass Interface was the key—a bridge between their current timeline and the alternate realities she sought to explore.

Her thoughts drifted back to the conversation with Raj. His support and understanding had fortified her resolve. They were both aware of the risks, the geopolitical implications, and the ever-looming presence of external threats. But beneath all that, there was a shared belief in the transformative power of their work.

Raina's past was marked by moments of regret and missed opportunities. She had often wondered what could have been different if only she had the chance to rewrite certain chapters of her life. This project, this groundbreaking technology, offered that chance—not just for her, but for humanity as a whole. The ability to manipulate timelines, to create parallel universes, could revolutionize their understanding of reality and existence.

She immersed herself in her work, her mind racing with equations and theories. The notebook she had shared with Raj lay open beside her, filled with annotations and refinements. Each line of code, each adjustment to the interface, brought her one step closer to her goal. She could almost see the alternate realities unfolding before her eyes—worlds where different choices had been made, where the trajectory of lives had taken entirely new directions.

But Raina knew this wasn't just a scientific endeavor. It was a deeply personal quest. The past held pain and loss, but it also held the seeds of potential futures. By altering the fabric of time, she hoped to create a tapestry where the threads of her life intertwined in new and unexpected ways. It was a chance to heal old wounds, to discover new possibilities, and to transcend the limitations of their current reality.

As dawn approached, Raina felt a sense of clarity and purpose unlike any she had ever known. The path ahead was fraught with challenges, but she was ready to face them. The Photonic Mass Interface was more than just a technological breakthrough; it was a beacon of hope, a gateway to a future where the past could be reimagined and the present transformed.

She glanced at a photo on her desk—an old snapshot of her family, taken during happier times. It was a reminder of what she had lost and what she still hoped to achieve. With a determined smile, Raina turned back to her work, her fingers flying across the keyboard. She was on the brink of something extraordinary, and nothing would stand in her way.

Raina was ready. Ready to devote herself to this technology, ready to change the past, and ready to create a new future. The parallel universe paradox wasn't just a theoretical concept; it was a reality waiting to be born, and she was its architect. Together with Raj, she would navigate the complexities of their mission, driven by a shared vision of a world where the possibilities were as infinite as the stars.

With a deep breath, Raina opened her notebook and began sketching out the next phase of her work. There was no turning back now. The journey into the paradox had begun.

END IS STILL FAR

The story of Raina and Raj is far from over, as their connection deepens and the stakes continue to rise. Their personal and professional lives become further entangled, creating a complex web of emotions and challenges. As they push forward with the development of the Photonic Mass Interface, their relationship will face critical tests. Will they be able to maintain the delicate balance between their feelings and their responsibilities? And what will be the ultimate cost of their devotion to this revolutionary technology?

Raj's family will undoubtedly be affected by his involvement with Raina and the high-stakes nature of their work. The tension between his professional commitments and his personal life will grow, raising questions about the impact on his marriage and children. Can Raj protect his family from the dangers that now surround him, or will the pressure drive them apart?

The Chinese, having already demonstrated a keen interest in the Photonic Mass Interface, will stop at nothing to secure the technology for their own purposes. Their involvement will escalate, leading to a high-stakes game of espionage and sabotage. Will they be able to infiltrate the project further, or will Raina and Raj outmaneuver them in this race for technological dominance?

As for the Photonic Mass Interface itself, its success will have far-reaching consequences. If Raina and Raj can complete its development, the technology could revolutionize the future of trans movements, opening the door to manipulating time, space, and human existence. But the path ahead is fraught with uncertainties. Will the interface work as intended, or will unforeseen complications arise?

All these questions and more will unfold in **"The Indeterminate Relationship: Part 2."** The journey of Raina and Raj will continue, taking them deeper into a world of intrigue, ambition, and emotional complexity. As they navigate the challenges of love, loyalty, and the future of humanity, the answers to these mysteries will determine the fate of not only their relationship but also the course of technological progress itself.

NOTE OF THANKS

To all the readers who have journeyed through *The Indeterminate Relationship*, I extend my deepest gratitude. Your support, curiosity, and engagement have brought life to this story, and it has been an honor to share this exploration of love, loyalty, and ambition with you.

Writing this novel has been a deeply personal experience, and knowing that it resonated with you makes the journey all the more rewarding. Your reflections, thoughts, and patience as the narrative unfolded have meant the world to me.

As the story of Raina and Raj continues into the next part, I hope it stirs your imagination, keeps you on the edge of your seat, and evokes the emotional connections that have guided their journey thus far.

Thank you for being a part of this experience. I look forward to continuing this journey with you in *The Indeterminate Relationship: Part 2*.

With gratitude,
Bhuvi

Short Note On Each Of Bhuvi's Novels Notes From People

The Burning Desire

This novel weaves a tale of passion, ambition, and the complexities of human relationships. It explores the journey of its characters as they navigate their desires and the challenges that come with pursuing their dreams. The narrative delves into themes of love, betrayal, and the profound impact of choices made in the heat of the moment, ultimately revealing how burning desires can shape destinies.

Journey to NDA

In this inspiring story, the protagonist embarks on a transformative journey to the National Defence Academy (NDA). Through dedication, discipline, and perseverance, they face numerous challenges that test their resolve. The novel captures the spirit of camaraderie, the rigors of military training, and the values instilled in future leaders. It serves as a reminder that the path to greatness is often fraught with obstacles, but with determination, one can overcome them to achieve their dreams.

Madhulika

Madhulika is a reflective exploration of life's lessons, both admirable and painful. The protagonist's journey evokes a mix of laughter and introspection as they navigate relationships, personal growth, and the quest for understanding. The story weaves together moments of joy and sorrow, ultimately revealing how experiences shape our identities and perspectives. Through Madhulika's journey, readers are invited to reflect on their own lives and the lessons that come with them.

Each of these novels encapsulates Bhuvi's unique storytelling style, blending rich character development with thought-provoking themes. As readers delve into these stories, they are sure to find themselves immersed in captivating narratives that resonate on multiple levels.

www.ingramcontent.com/pod-product-compliance
Lightning Source LLC
Chambersburg PA
CBHW021553150726

47990CB00006B/2529